LAY THE MOUNTAINS LOW

THE PLAINSMEN SERIES BY TERRY C. JOHNSTON

LAY THE MOUNTAINS LOW

The Flight of the Nez Perce from Idaho
and the Battle of the Big Hole,
August 9–10, 1877

TERRY C. JOHNSTON

ST. MARTIN'S PRESS   NEW YORK

Book design by Victoria Kuskowski

Library of Congress Cataloging-in-Publication Data

Johnston, Terry C.
  Lay the mountains low : the flight of the Nez Perce from Idaho and the Battle of
the Big Hole, August 9–10, 1877 / Terry C. Johnston.—1st ed.
      p.   cm.
    ISBN 0-312-26189-6
    1. Nez Percâ Indians—Wars, 1877—Fiction.   2. Indians of North America—
Montana—Fiction.   3. Indians of North America—Idaho—Fiction.   4. Big Hole,
Battle of the, 1877—Fiction.   5. Nez Percâ Indians—Fiction.   6. Montana—
Fiction.   7. Idaho—Fiction.   I. Title.

PS3560.O392 L3 2000
813'.54—dc21

                                                                    00-024201

First Edition: June 2000

10   9   8   7   6   5   4   3   2   1

Across the last fourteen years

as we collaborated on one

historically authentic and accurate

book cover after another,

we have forged a timeless and unbreakable bond

of friendship and camaraderie . . .

yet while I have been blessed to share his artwork

with my readers around the world,

I am even more honored this man

calls me friend—

I lovingly dedicate this heart-wrenching novel

of the turning point in the Nez Perce War to

that good ol' Virginia boy who is without peer:

my cover artist,

Lou Glanzman.

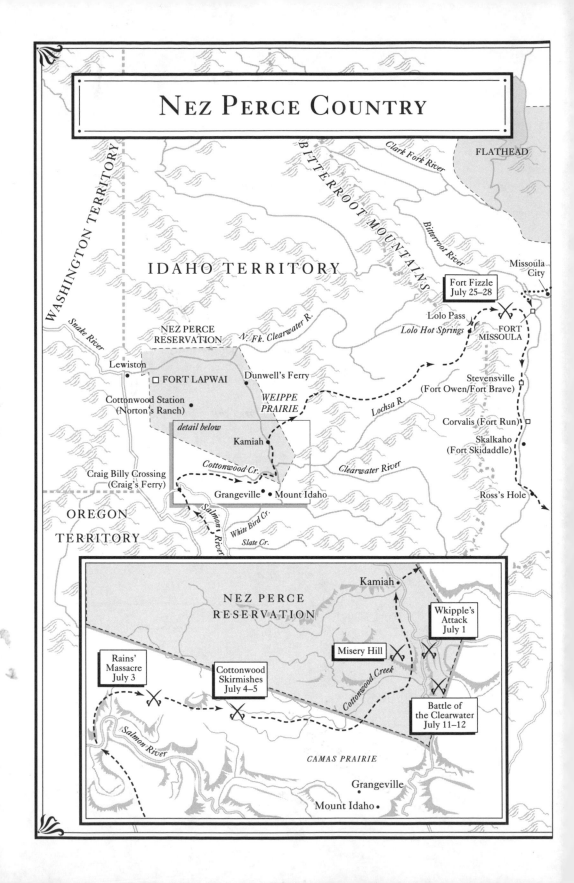

NEZ PERCE COUNTRY

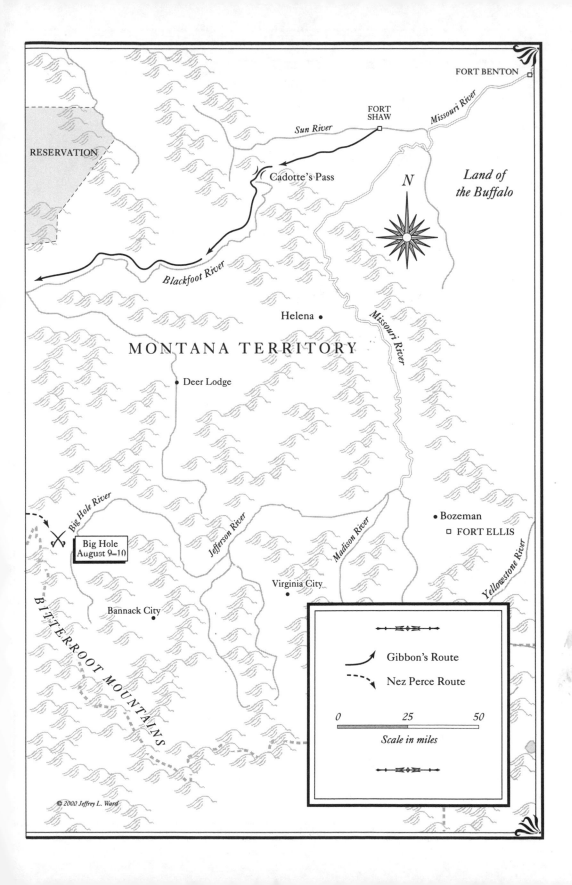

FORT BENTON

FORT SHAW

Sun River

Missouri River

RESERVATION

Cadotte's Pass

Land of the Buffalo

N

Blackfoot River

Helena •

Missouri River

MONTANA TERRITORY

• Deer Lodge

Big Hole River

Big Hole
August 9–10

Jefferson River

Madison River

• Bozeman
□ FORT ELLIS

Yellowstone River

Virginia City •

B I T T E R R O O T   M O U N T A I N S

Bannack City •

Gibbon's Route

Nez Perce Route

0   25   50

Scale in miles

© 2000 Jeffrey L. Ward

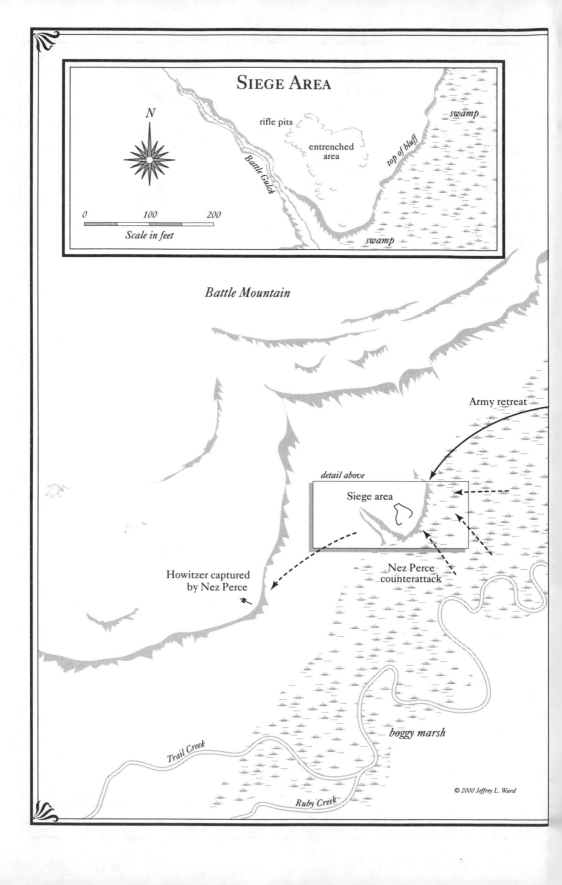

SIEGE AREA

N

rifle pits

entrenched
area

swamp

Battle Gulch

top of bluff

swamp

0   100   200

Scale in feet

Battle Mountain

Army retreat

detail above

Siege area

Nez Perce
counterattack

Howitzer captured
by Nez Perce

boggy marsh

Trail Creek

Ruby Creek

© 2000 Jeffrey L. Ward

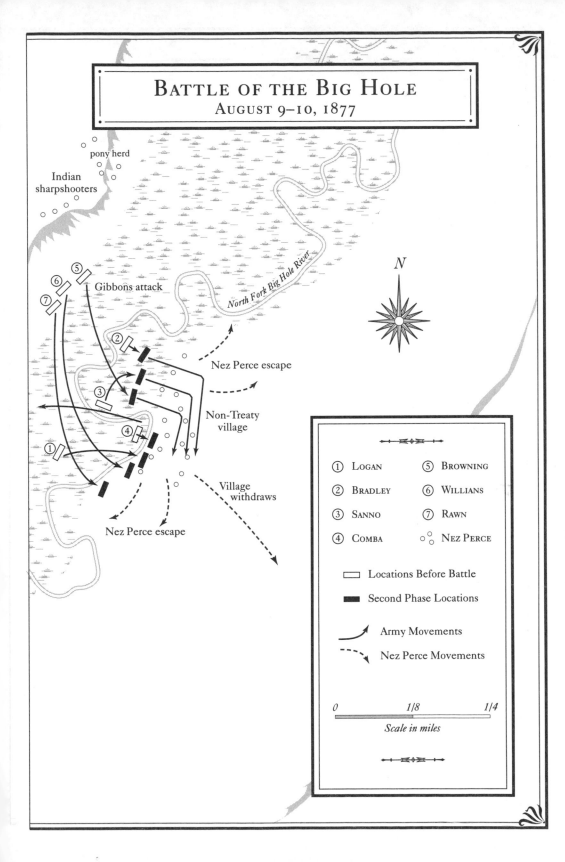

BATTLE OF THE BIG HOLE
AUGUST 9–10, 1877

pony herd

Indian sharpshooters

Gibbons attack

North Fork Big Hole River

N

Nez Perce escape

Non-Treaty village

Village withdraws

Nez Perce escape

① LOGAN   ⑤ BROWNING

② BRADLEY   ⑥ WILLIANS

③ SANNO   ⑦ RAWN

④ COMBA   NEZ PERCE

▭ Locations Before Battle

▬ Second Phase Locations

↗ Army Movements

⇢ Nez Perce Movements

0   1/8   1/4

Scale in miles

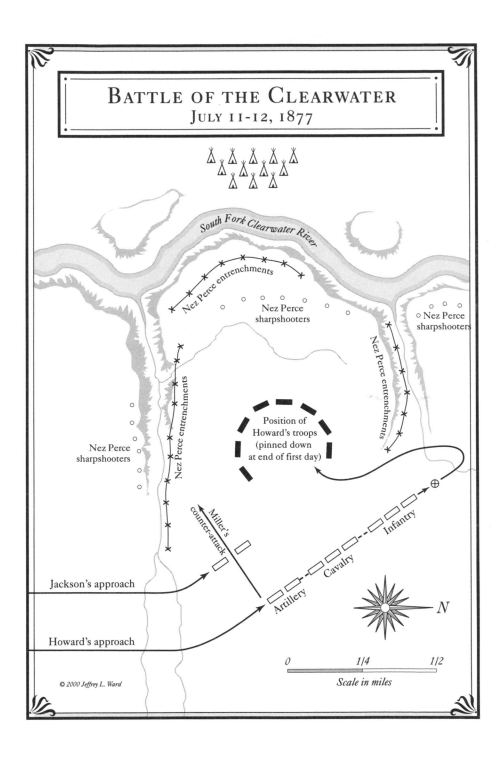

BATTLE OF THE CLEARWATER
JULY 11-12, 1877

South Fork Clearwater River

Nez Perce entrenchments

Nez Perce
sharpshooters

Nez Perce
sharpshooters

Nez Perce entrenchments

Nez Perce
sharpshooters

Nez Perce entrenchments

Position of
Howard's troops
(pinned down
at end of first day)

Miller's
counter-attack

Infantry

Cavalry

Artillery

Jackson's approach

Howard's approach

N

© 2000 Jeffrey L. Ward

0   1/4   1/2

Scale in miles

CAST OF CHARACTERS

CIVILIANS

Emily F. FitzGerald
Elizabeth FitzGerald
Bert FitzGerald
Jennie Norton
Elizabeth Osborn
Norman Gould
John B. Monteith
Erwin C. Watkins
"Captain" Tom Page
Benjamin F. Potts
Washington "Dutch" Holmes
Dave Ousterholt
Luther P. "Lew" Wilmot
"Captain" Benjamin F. Morris
Eugene Tallmadge Wilson
"Captain" James L. Cearly
P. C. Malin
Benjamin Penny
William Foster
Frank Parker
Jack Carleton
Chauncey Barbour
"Captain" John Humble
"Sergeant" Joseph Baker
Peter H. Ready
Frank A. Fenn
Henry C. Johnson
Cassius M. "Cash" Day
D. H. Howser
Alonzo B. Leland
F. Joseph "Joe" Moore
Charles Johnson
Henry W. Croasdaile
Williams George
George M. Shearer
Loyal P. (L. P.) Brown
H. C. "Hurdy Gurdy" Brown
John J. Manuel
Peter Matte
Thomas A. Sutherland

Benjamin Norton
Hill Norton
Lynn Bowers
Helen Walsh
George Greer
Peter Ronan
"Captain" William Hunter
"Captain" J. W. Elliott
William Watson
J. A. Miller
"Colonel" Edward McConville
John Atkinson
George Hunter
John McPherson
George Riggins
Elias Darr
"Laughing" Williams
James T. Silverwood
E. A. Kenney
W. J. Stephens
"Captain" Darius B. (D. B.) Randall
Frank D. Vansise
Ephraim J. Bunker
Pete Bremen
James Buchanan
Charley Case
Benjamin F. Evans
Mrs. Chamberlin
Peter Minturn
Paul Guiterman
Sarah Brown
Maggie Manuel
Albert Benson
John W. Crooks
"Captain" Orlando "Rube" Robbins
John Crooks, Jr.
William Silverthorne
Alexander Matte
Dr. John Morris
Charley Crooks

Dan Crooks
Arthur "Ad"/"Admiral" Chapman
Henry Buck
Fred Buck
Joe Pardee
"Captain" John B. Catlin
Wesley Little
H. S. Bostwick
Campbell Mitchell
William H. Edwards
Jerry Wallace
"Captain" John L. Humble
John Buckhouse
Reverend W. T. Flowers
Amos Buck

Jerry Fahy
Myron Lockwood
Father Anthony Ravalli
Joe Blodgett
Hugh Kirkendall
"Captain" William R. Logan
William Woodcock
Nelse McGilliam
John Miller
Alfred Cave
Wilson B. Harlan
Luther Johnson
Tom Sherrill
"Bunch" Sherrill
Mr. Bonny

MILITARY

Major General Irwin McDowell
Captain Birney Keeler

Brigadier General Oliver Otis
  Howard / "Cut-Off Arm" /
  "Never Going to Fight Until
  Tomorrow"

First U. S. Cavalry

Major George B. Sanford
Captain David Perry—F Troop
Captain Joel G. Trimble—
  H Troop
Captain Henry E. Winters—
  E Troop
Captain Stephen Gerard
  Whipple—L Troop
Captain James B. Jackson—
  B Troop
First Lieutenant Edwin H.
  Shelton—L Troop
First Lieutenant Albert G. Forse—
  E Troop
First Lieutenant George R.
  Bacon—K Troop
Second Lieutenant William Russell
  Parnell—H Troop
Second Lieutenant Sevier
  McClellan Rains—L Troop
Second Lieutenant William H.
  Miller—E Troop

Major John Wesley Green
First Sergeant Oliver Sutherland
  (Sean Dennis Geoghegan)—B
  Troop
Sergeant Bernard Simpson—L
  Troop
Sergeant Isidor Schneider—H
  Troop
Sergeant Charles Lampman—E
  Troop
Trumpeter Frank A. Marshall—H
  Troop
Farrier John Drugan—H Troop
Private David Carroll—L Troop
Private George H. Dinteman—L
  Troop
Private Otto H. Richter—L Troop
Private William Roche—E Troop
Private Franklin Moody—
  L Troop
Second Lieutenant Thomas T.
  Knox—H Troop

First Sergeant Michael
McCarthy—H Troop
Private Patrick Quinn—E Troop
Private John Burk—E Troop

Private Charles E. Fowler—
H Troop
Private Frederick Meyer—L Troop
Private Daniel Ryan—E Troop

Second U. S. Cavalry

Sergeant Edward Page—L Troop

Fourth U. S. Artillery

Captain Marcus P. Miller—
commanding artillery battalion
Captain Eugene A. Bancroft—
M Battery
Captain Charles B.
Throckmorton—M Battery

Captain Harry C. Cushing—C
Battery
Captain George B. Rodney—D
Battery
Second Lieutenant Harrison G.
Otis—E Battery

Seventh U. S. Infantry

Colonel John Gibbon—regiment
commander
Captain Charles C. Rawn—I
Company
Captain William Logan—A
Company
Captain James M. W. Sanno—G
Company
Captain Richard Comba—D
Company
Captain George L. Browning—G
Company
First Lieutenant Joshua W.
Jacobs—regimental quartermaster
First Lieutenant William L.
English—I Company
First Lieutenant Charles A.
Coolidge—A Company
First Lieutenant James H.
Bradley—B Company
First Lieutenant Charles A.
Woodruff—K Company
(aide-de-camp to Colonel
Gibbon)
Second Lieutenant Francis
Woodbridge—A Company
Lieutenant Tom Andrews—A
Company

Lieutenant Levi F. Burnett—
Gibbon's aide at Fort Shaw
First Sergeant Patrick Rogan—A
Company
Sergeant John Raferty—A Company
Sergeant Michael Hogan—I
Company
Sergeant John W. H. Frederick—G
Company
Sergeant Patrick C. Daly—D
Company
Sergeant Mildon H. Wilson—I
Company
Corporal Charles N. Loynes—I
Company
Corporal Robert E. Sale—G
Company
Corporal Socrates Drummond
Private Charles Alberts—A
Company
Private George Leher—A
Company
Private Homer Coon—G Company
Private John O. Bennett—B
Company
Private Malcolm McGregor—G
Company
Private John H. Goale—G Company

Twenty-first Infantry

Major Edwin C. Mason—
Department Inspector General,
Howard's Chief of Staff
Captain Evan Miles—infantry battalion commander
Captain William F. Spurgin—
commander, pioneer/engineer
company
Captain William H. Boyle—G
Company
Captain Robert Pollock—D
Company

First Lieutenant Robert H.
Fletcher—acting assistant adjutant general
First Lieutenant Fred H. E.
Ebstein—regimental and column
quartermaster
Lieutenant James A. Haughey—H
Company
Lieutenant Harry Bailey—B
Company
Private Francis Winters—B
Company

Howard's Staff

Captain Lawrence S. Babbitt
First Lieutenant Melville C.
Wilkinson
Second Lieutenant Guy Howard
Second Lieutenant Charles
Erskine Scott Wood
Colonel John Gibbon—commanding, Seventh U. S. Infantry

Surgeon Jenkins A. ("John")
FitzGerald—Fort Lapwai
Surgeon George M. Sternberg—
Fort Walla Walla
Assistant Surgeon William R. Hall

TREATY NEZ PERCE

John Hill
Tom Hill
James Lawyer
Archie Lawyer
James Reuben
Luke Billy
Robinson Minthon

Yuwishakaikit
Joe Albert / Elaskolatat
John Levi / "Captain John"/
Sheared Wolf
Abraham Brooks
Delaware Jim / Jim Simonds

NON-TREATY BANDS *Nee-Me-Poo*

Yellow Wolf / *Hemene Moxmox*
Old Yellow Wolf
Wemastahtus
Teminisiki
Horse Blanket / *Seekumses Kunnin*
Elm Limb / *Alahmoot*
Paktilek
Yiyik Wasumwah
Tomyunmene
Tommino

Going Across / *Wayakat*
Over the Point / *Teeweeyownah*
Three Feathers
Hair Combed Over Eyes / *Wottolen*
Weesculatat (Wounded Mouth /
Mimpow Owyeen)
White Cloud / *Sewattis Hihhih*
Five Wounds / *Pahkatos Owyeen*
Rainbow / *Wahchumyus*
Kulkulsuitim

Poker Joe / Lean Elk /
  Wa-wook-ke-ya Was Sauw / Joe Hale
Joseph / *Heinmot* (White Thunder)
Ta-ma-al-we-non-my / Driven Before
  a Cold Storm
Sun Necklace ("Yellow Bull" /
  Chuslum Moxmox)
Wounded Head / *Husis Owyeen*
No Feet / *Seeskoomkee*
Black Raven / *Nennin Chekoostin*
Strong Eagle / *Tipyahlahnah
  Kapskaps*
Shot Leg / *Tahkoopen*
Eagle Robe / *Tipyahlanah Siskon*
Shore Crossing / *Wahlitits*
Smoker / *Dookiyoon*
Red Moccasin Tops / *Sarpsis Ilppil*
Burning Coals / *Semu*
Eagle-from-the-Light
Black Foot
Mean Man / *Howwallits*
White Bull
(Josiah) Red Wolf
Rattle on Blanket /
  Lakochets Kunnin
Red Heart / *Temme Ilppilp*
Chee-Nah
Dropping from a Cliff /
  Tenahtahkal Weyun
Stripes Turned Down /
  Ketalkpoosmin
Log / *Weweetsa*
Bighorn Bow / *Tahwis Takaitat*
No Heart / *Zya Timenna*
Grizzly Bear Youth /
  Hohots Elotoht

Ollokot/ the Frog
Arrowhead / *Etemiere Aihits Palojami*
  / Fair Land
Red Elk
Toohoolhoolzote
Helping Another / *Penahwenonmi*
Pile of Clouds
Fire Body / *Otstotpoo*
Looking Glass / *Alalmiatakanin*
Bird Alighting / *Peopeo Tholekt*
White Bird
Red Spy / *Seeyakoon Ilppilp* / wife of
  Wahlitits—no recorded name
Swan Necklace /
  Wetyetmas Wahyakt
Grizzly Bear Blanket /
  Yoomstis Kunnin
Lone Bird / *Peopeo Ipsewahk*
Natalekin
About Asleep / *Eelahweeman*
Young White Bird
Dog / *Jeekunkun*
Suhm-Keen
Wahnistas Aswetesk
Sun Tied / *Weyatnahtoo Latat*
Calf of Leg / *Pitpillooheen*
Earth Blanket / *Wattes Kunnin*
Light in the Mountain / *Espowyes
  Quiloishkish*
Owhi (Yakima)
Horn Hide Dresser / *Tepsus*
Amos
Two Moons / *Lepeet Hessemdooks*
Going Out / *Otskai*
Kowtoliks
Five Fogs / *Pahka Pahtahank*

PALOUSE

Red Echo / *Hahtalekin*

Bald Head / Shorn Head /
  Huishuishkute

FLATHEAD

Charlot

Pierre

BANNOCK

Buffalo Horn

I would have given my own life I could have undone the killing of white men by my people. I blame young men and I blame the white men. I blame General Howard for not giving my people time to get their stock away from Wallowa. I do not acknowledge that he had the right to order me to leave Wallowa at any time. I deny that either my father or myself ever sold that land. It may never again be our home, but my father sleeps there, and I love it as I love my mother. I left there, hoping to avoid bloodshed.

—*Joseph*

The Rains encounter was a small but sweeping victory for the Nez Perces. Coming on the heels of their success over the army at White Bird Canyon, it had the effect of inspiring them to continue in their course. It impacted the army negatively, not only through the loss of Rains and his men, but it prevented Howard from attaining the upper hand in the war and ending it quickly, while simultaneously contributing to the building public skepticism about army capabilities.

—*Jerome A. Greene*
The U. S. Army and the Nee-Mee-Poo Crisis of 1877

If Howard had been as bold [at the Clearwater] as General Gibbon [was at the Big Hole] we might have been all taken, alhtough we intended to fight to the last.

—*White Bird*

The Battle of the Clearwater was indisputably a watershed in the army's campaign against the Nez Perces. By not pressing them in their retreat from the village, General Howard lost both the initiative and an opportunity to finally curb the nontreaty Nez Perces and end the war.

—*Jerome A. Greene*

In retrospect, the Nez Perces' parochial perspective of the war, and their insensibility to comprehending the scale and span of the United States government's resistance to [their flight from their homes in Idaho Territory to the Big Hole in Montana Territory], became key ingredients in their ultimate tragedy.

—*Jerome A. Greene*

AUTHOR'S FOREWORD

Before you begin reading this book, I want you to take a moment to consider that the story you hold in your hands is entirely true.

While I'm sure you realize that I have constructed dialogue from a myriad of historical documents to make this story leap off the page with a sense of immediacy, I have striven to capture each person's individual character in their manner of speech. Rest assured that I haven't fabricated a single one of the scenes that follow this introduction. Every incident happened when and where and how I have written it. Every one of the characters you will come to know actually lived, perhaps died, during these pivotal weeks during the Nez Perce War of 1877.

After my previous fourteen *Plainsmen* novels, millions of you already have an abiding faith in me, a belief that what you're going to read is accurate and truly authentic.

But for those of you thumbing through your first Terry C. Johnston book, let me make this one very crucial promise to you: If I show one of these fascinating historical characters in a particular scene, then you best believe that character was there—when it happened, where it happened. I promise you, despite the overwhelmingly popular and politically correct notions long held by most people, this is how the tragedy of the Nez Perce War did unfold.

Truth is, I could have written a book nearly twice as long as this if I had explored the complex historical background of the old treaties and how they were broken after gold was discovered deep in Nez Perce country, if I had begun reciting in chapter and verse all the intrusions by whites where they were not allowed by the early treaties, relating to you that seductive lure of alcohol and firearms on the young warriors; writing of the rapes and murders committed against those Nez Perce bands helplessly watching as their old way of life was trampled underfoot right before their eyes, not to mention the government's feeble efforts to keep a lid on each deplorable incident after the fact. . . .

But, for all that detailed background I didn't cram into these three novels I'm writing on the Nez Perce War, the reader can learn every detail he or she wants to know in the following books:

I Will Fight No More Forever, by Merrill D. Beal

The Flight of the Nez Perce, by Mark H. Brown

The Nez Perce Tribesmen of the Columbia Plateau, by Francis Haines

The Nez Perce Indians and the Opening of the Northwest, by Alvin M. Joseph, Jr.

As for my story—beginning with the outbreak of the war as I told it in *Cries from the Earth*—I dispensed with all that oft-confusing historical background because you can learn it far better elsewhere . . . and because I prefer to plop you right down into the middle of this tragic conflict.

As you are drawn back in time and reading the pages of my story, you may well wonder: What are these brief news articles that appear here and there at the beginning of certain chapters or scenes? Keep in mind that those clippings aren't the fruits of my creative imagination. Rather, they are ripped right from the front pages of the newspapers read by living, breathing people in that summer of 1877.

One more sidelight before you start what will surely be one of the most fascinating rides of your life—the letters that Emily FitzGerald, wife of surgeon John FitzGerald, writes home to her mother from Fort Lapwai are real, too. Transcribed verbatim for you, every last word of those letters make them simple, heartfelt messages from a woman who finds herself trapped squarely at ground zero, right in the middle of an Indian war.

I hope Emily's letters, along with those timely newspaper clippings, will lend an air of immediacy to this gripping tale that every other book on the Nez Perce War has not.

As you make your way through this story, page by page, many of you might start to worry when you find this tale missing our intrepid Irishman, Seamus Donegan. Be strong of heart! In the next volume—*The Broken Hoop*—Seamus; his wife, Samantha; and their son, Colin, will migrate from Fort Laramie in the spring of 1877, making their way north to Fort Robinson, where they will find themselves on center stage for the last months of Crazy Horse's life. When his old friend Colonel Nelson A. Miles marches his Fifth U. S. Infantry north from Tongue River in pursuit of the Nez Perce fleeing for Canada (that third and final act in this tragedy), the Irishman will be along . . . as a brutal winter storm and the army descend upon the Bears Paw Mountains—catching the Non-Treaty bands just forty miles short of the Old Woman's Country.

As you saddle up and begin this ride with me, I want to remind you that every scene you are about to read actually happened. Every one of these characters was real—and they were there to walk that hallowed ground . . . to live or die in what fading glory still belonged to the Nez Perce in a damned and dirty little war.

I couldn't have made up this remarkably intricate and tragic story if I'd tried. I simply don't consider myself that good a writer.

Second Lieutenant Sevier M. Rains, 1876, USMA (photo credit: United States Military Academy)

Above: Yellow Wolf (photo credit: Montana Historical Society)

Below: Cottonwood Ranch and Hotel (photo credit: *Sun Magazine*, San Francisco)

Right: Looking Glass (photo credit: National Anthropological Archives, Smithsonian Institution, #2953–A)

Bottom Left: Dr. Jenkins (John) A. FitzGerald (photo credit): *An Army Doctor's Wife on the Frontier*, used by permission of the University of Pittsburgh Press)

Bottom Right: Colonel John Gibbon, Seventh U.S. Infantry (photo credit: Montana Historical Society)

LAY THE
MOUNTAINS
LOW

PROLOGUE

—◄◆►—

20 JUNE 1877

URSING THE RISING SUN UNDER HIS BREATH, FIRST SERGEANT MICHAEL McCarthy ground the heels of both hands into his gummy, crusted eyes.

Already this morning the little settlement of Grangeville was slowly stirring—not just those soldiers and civilians who stood watch at the barricades for the approach of Joseph's Nez Perce warriors, but those men rekindling fires, women stirring up breakfast, and even the few children adding their cheery, innocent voices to the coming of this new day.

Squinting overhead, the Canadian-born McCarthy found a clearing sky. Far better than the low, leaden clouds that had hovered above them almost from the moment Captain David Perry had led them out of Fort Lapwai after the marauding Non-Treaty bands.

Perry. Just thinking about the man made McCarthy hawk up the night-gather clinging at the back of his throat. Now there was a coward weighed down beneath a captain's bars! There wasn't a goddamned reason they should have left more than a third of their command down in that valley of White Bird Canyon. A good officer, a brave commander, could have seized control of those wavering troopers, halted their wild retreat before it ever got started. . . .

The thirty-two-year-old soldier hung his head and took a deep breath as he clenched his eyes shut. McCarthy remembered—doubting he ever would forget—the sights he had left behind him on that battleground. Last man out that he was. The last to crawl up the 3,000 feet of White Bird Canyon . . . the valley floor behind him littered with dead and wounded comrades, swarming with Nez Perce horsemen like an attack of summer wasps boiling out of their nest.

Perry had gone and jabbed a big stick right into that nest. And when there was nothing left for any of them to do but turn about and high-tail it back up the canyon wall, Captain David Perry was powerless to control the panic. Damn, but Michael couldn't blame those poor enlisted weeds: Why would any of them want to stop, turn around, and start fighting anew for a commander like David Perry? Not when the captain had marched his bone-weary men down through the dark toward an enemy no one knew a god-blame-it thing about, every one of his hundred soldiers riding too-tired and ill-fed horses.

"They wasn't ready to fight," he grumbled under his breath now as he dragged over the first brown boot. For a moment he caressed the soft, saddle-soaped texture of the tall, mule-eared boot top. *God bless sutler Rudolph,* he thought. *Godbless'im, Lord.*

The afternoon after First Sergeant Michael McCarthy had been discovered and brought in by those two civilian volunteers from out near Johnson's ranch, near halfway between the White Bird divide and the settlement of Grangeville, Rudolph had graciously presented McCarthy with a pair of real leather boots to take the place of those ill-fitting rubber miner's boots the sergeant had discovered in an abandoned cabin on his way over the divide to the Camas Prairie. Once more, Michael knew how the Lord doth provide!

Left behind by the rest of those hardy old files bringing up the rear of the frantic retreat, McCarthy had lain there on the slope, playing dead until the screaming warriors thundered past. Only then did he quickly roll into the willow and wild rose lining the banks of White Bird Creek, slipping into the water so that only his head was showing there beneath the low-hanging brush. After waiting out the comings and going of the warriors searching for any wounded soldiers and looting the bodies of his poor dead comrades, it was no wonder the icy-cold water had soaked his regulation boots through and through. Soles falling away from lasts, stitches unraveling. Utterly worthless: just like near every other piece of equipment this god-blame-it army gave its soldiers to use. Boots that never would get him up that slope he had studied from between the leafy willow—only to find that he'd been discovered by a fat Indian squaw riding past on her pony.

How his heart had frozen when the fat one called over an old man—pointing to the clump of willow where McCarthy lay hidden. He had pulled out his service revolver and prepared to take as many of them with him as he could before he was killed. But . . . search as he did, the old man didn't spot him. He rode off with the woman.

In the quiet where he could hear his own heart surging in his ears, McCarthy quickly tore off his campaign hat, slipped out of his navy blue fatigue blouse with its telltale gold stripes. If he'd dared to tug off his light blue wool britches with their wide brassy stripe running down the outside . . . but he knew he would need them in his run for freedom. Wasn't no man going to make it to the settlements near naked!

Besides the gift of those knee-high boots, sutler Rudolph had presented the sergeant with a pair of leather gloves and a new felt hat—gray as the skies had been the last three days.

"You're a honest-to-God hero," Rudolph had announced to the crowd when he presented his gifts to the newly arrived McCarthy. "All you soldiers are heroes to us!"

And then the gathering of some forty men, women, and children huddled behind an upright stockade, which they had erected right around Grange Hall, huzzahed as if they had just been delivered from the hoary grip of death itself. Just the way Michael McCarthy had been scooped up by some angel and carried out of that valley of death, deposited at the top of White Bird divide, where he made three wrong turns and ended up wandering the heights for far longer than he should have.

When those two soldiers brought the ravenous McCarthy to the barricades, his nose caught the whiff of an enticing perfume. Someone had beans on the boil. "White dodgers!" he had exclaimed as he vaulted off the back end of that tired cavalry horse, lumbering across the breastworks for that seductive pot. First things first. He'd look for familiar faces from his H Company once his belly was full. Enough time to make reacquaintance with his weeds what made it out of that Injun fight with their hides intact.

"Sweet, sweet Joseph and Mary," he murmured again, clenching his eyes as he rocked onto his knees, preparing to roll up his blankets. Would he never forget the sight of Corporal Roman D. Lee being dragged from his horse, the entire front of his blue britches turned black with blood gushing from that bullet to the groin? Would he ever be able to blot out the nightmare of watching Lee stumble away from his handlers like a drunken sailor newly arrived on dry land, wandering off into that milling, confusing, maddening maze of confused men and frightened horses? Would he never be rid of watching the corporal unknowingly weave and lunge on down that emerald grassy slope—right for the enemy's lines?

At sundown each of the last two nights, Second Lieutenant William Russell Parnell had come whistling up the company, calling out men to post a rotation for night guard. Too much darkness, too much quiet, too damned much time each night on watch . . . time alone to think and remember.

He took a deep breath and pushed an unruly lock of his dark auburn hair from his eyes, telling himself such haunting was the lot of a soldier. Be he an Irishman like McCarthy or one of those pig-swilling Germans, a soldier was bound to lose friends. Maybeso, it wasn't a good thing for a sergeant to have him any friends. Only officers above him and enlisted boyos below. Maybe there was a damned good reason officers never talked to their weeds— communicating only through the noncoms like McCarthy. That way an officer didn't have to care who was thrown into the fray, who would never ride back with the company.

When McCarthy gave orders to H Company, it was with a voice still very thick with that Newfoundland Irish heritage of his. As soon as he was old enough to leave home and strike out on his own, McCarthy had wandered south from Canada, spending a short time in Vermont before migrating down to Boston. In that good Irish town he had knocked around a bit before he landed steady work as a printer's devil. A year later when the Civil War broke out, he was only fifteen—too young to enlist, having to content himself by following the war with every new edition or extra of the Boston paper.

By the time the Southern states had been defeated and herded back into the Union fold, McCarthy had wearied of the acrid stench of printer's ink etching every wrinkle and crevice of his hands, chuffing down the street to inscribe his mark on a five-year enlistment. Sending him west to Jefferson Barracks near St. Louis, the army trained him to be a horseman, then promptly shipped him off to a First Cavalry outfit down near the Mexican border to fight Apaches. Wasn't long before they transferred McCarthy, now wearing a corporal's stripes, along with some of his mates, all hustled north to Oregon country, where they ended up chasing half a hundred poor Modocs around and through the Lava Beds for the better part of a year.

Fact was, McCarthy had been in on the chase and capture of the Modoc leader, Captain Jack. A heart-wrenching tragedy that was, McCarthy thought many times since—how the chief's friends, advisers, and headmen had all turned on him. Sad, too, that most of those back-stabbing traitors went free while Jack swung at the end of a short rope.

He smelled tobacco all of a sudden. McCarthy glanced at the knot of men gathered on their haunches around a small fire, most of their number smoking their first bowl of the day. His heart seized with the sudden recollection of their blind descent into the valley of the White Bird behind Perry, ordered to halt and wait until it was light enough to make their advance on the village. Up and down the ranks of those two companies, five officers, and more than a dozen Nez Perce friendlies conscripted as trackers the order was given that no pipes be lit.

Later, as the horses snuffled and the men grumbled every time they were nudged to keep them awake in the cold, damp darkness, McCarthy spotted the bright, minute flare of the sulphur-headed lucifer. The sergeant had bounded over, ready to throttle and choke the stupid weed who was trying to light his goddamned pipe.

The match had flared for but the space of three heartbeats before McCarthy got it extinguished. Then thought nothing more of it until they all heard the off-key, muffled call of a coyote. Its eerie, echoing cry had raised the reddish hair on the back of his neck. A few of the old files had known right then what was in store for them come first light.

That weren't no coyote. Some Nez Perce sentry had seen the bloody burning match . . . and the bastards knew the soldiers had come for them—

"Sergeant! Sergeant!" called Trumpeter Frank A. Marshall as the soldier came trotting up the end of Grangeville's one long street, breathless.

As Marshall skidded to a halt right at McCarthy's toes, out of the trees to their left stepped the big German sergeant, Isidor Schneider. McCarthy liked the man—no matter that it was hard for McCarthy to understand his thick accent at times. Michael counted on the thick-hammed German to help him run H Company smoothly.

"Suck a breath, Private," the short, slim McCarthy reminded the trumpeter. "And tell me what orders you've got for us this fine morning."

McCarthy steeled himself, not sure he was ready for another of those assignments the officers always handed him alone—like picking a squad of steady men and holding off the screaming red heathens from that outcropping of rocks while the rest of Perry's command skeedaddled from the battlefield like banshees were nipping at their heels. Another god-blame-it suicide run—

"We're g-going b-back, Sergeant."

As a dozen or more of H Company's green-broke shavetail recruits inched closer, Farrier John Drugan lunged to a stop at Marshall's elbow. "Back? Whooo-eee! We're going back to our post?"

Marshall shook his head and swallowed, still struggling to catch his breath from his sprint over with the latest from Perry's headquarters.

"We're not going back to the fort?" McCarthy asked, sweeping one of the droopy, unkempt ends of his shaggy reddish-brown mustache away from his lips suddenly gone dry.

"No, Sergeant," the trumpeter confirmed steadily.

Michael was afraid to ask. He thought of friends and fellow soldiers already waiting for him at Fiddler's Green—the place in the great beyond where every good horse soldier went when his duty roster was up.

A drop of cold sweat slowly spilled down the course of McCarthy's spine, oozing into the crack of his ass. "Back where, Private?"

Pasty-faced, Marshall turned, pointed off to the southwest, toward the White Bird divide. "Going back . . . to the b-battlefield."

CHAPTER ONE

JUNE 21, 1877

HE HAD FOUGHT AGAINST THE CREAM OF THE CONFEDERACY AND CHASED, then hung, the leaders of the Modoc insurrection in southern Oregon years ago. So why did he find himself dreading this ride down into the canyon of White Bird Creek the way a frightened schoolboy would fear a midnight trek to a cemetery?

Deep in the marrow of him, Captain David Perry knew that what awaited him on that abandoned battlefield was far worse than anything a schoolboy might encounter in some haunted graveyard. Not only would he be forced to view the bloated, contorted bodies of those men he had led into the valley at dawn on the seventeenth of June, but he was coming to believe that he just might confront the restless, disembodied spirits of those soldiers who would forever walk that bloody ground.

If Brigadier General Howard, even that damnable, self-serving coward Trimble, didn't utter a public charge about his debacle in the valley of the White Bird, then Perry was afraid his greatest fear would come to pass: The ghosts of those men sacrificed to the Nez Perce would shriek aloud their charges of incompetence and timidity . . . if not outright cowardice.

Oh, the hours and days he had brooded over every deployment of his forces, every action of his company commanders, each tiny reaction of his own during the short, fierce fight since that damp morning when he had been tested and somehow found wanting. Had he committed his one-hundred-man force to battle without trustworthy intelligence, taking only the word of the civilian volunteers that the Nez Perce wouldn't dare stand and fight?

David Perry, post commander at nearby Fort Lapwai, simply could not shake the unrelenting sleeplessness his doubts awakened within his most private soul, nor rid himself of the constant horror he saw behind his eyelids every time he shut his eyes and attempted to squeeze out the respite of a little rest from each endless night. He wondered if he would ever find a way to rid himself of this haunting.

Like an arrow a man would release into the air, aimed directly over-head—an arrow that might well fall back toward earth to wound or even kill that bowman—Perry understood his hasty, ill-considered journey into the White Bird Canyon would one day return to be his undoing. But the captain fervently prayed this would not be that day.

Before he led his men south from Grangeville that Thursday morning, the twenty-first of June, Perry confided in those fellow officers who, with him, had survived their humiliating defeat on the White Bird.

"We'll make a reconnaissance as far as the top of the divide," he instructed them. "And stop where we began to descend into the valley on the seventeenth . . . halting where we can view the battlefield at a distance."

"We best keep our eyes skinned for them redskins," injected Arthur Chapman, a local rancher who was better known as Ad, bastardized from "Admiral," a name bestowed upon him for his uncanny ability to handle small craft on the region's swollen, raging rivers.

Perry turned to peer at that volunteer scout coming to a stop within the ring of officers. "You volunteering to lead us back across the ridge, Mr. Chapman?"

The tall civilian appeared to weigh that briefly, his eyes darting among the other soldiers who stood at Perry's elbows. Pushing some black hair out of his eyes, Chapman sighed. "I figger it's the decent thing to do, Colonel," he explained, using Perry's brevet, or honorary, rank earned during the Civil War. "But mind you, if them Injuns whupped us and drove your soldiers off once, they sure as hell can wipe you out now—they catch us in the open again."

Perry squinted his eyes, peering at that knot of horsemen who warily sat far off to the side of his column of blue-clad soldiers. "What of your recruitment efforts among the civilian populace, Mr. Chapman?"

"Maybe a dozen," the civilian replied. "No more'n that come along with me."

"That'll have to do—as many local citizens as you can muster." Perry did his best to sound upbeat. "Gentlemen, prepare your companies. We'll move out on our reconnaissance in thirty minutes."

Here at the top of the White Bird divide, the captain had halted his depleted, nervous command. Gathering both left and right at the front of Perry's column Chapman's civilians sat atop their horses, letting their animals blow. At their feet lay the steep slope Perry's doomed battalion had scrambled back up on the morning of 17 June. Only four short days ago.

His heart pounded in his chest. Surely the victorious Non-Treaty bands had abandoned the area.

"Don't see no smoke, Colonel," Chapman advised as he eased back to Perry's side.

Civilian George M. Shearer, a veteran of that all-too-brief White Bird battle, agreed, "Likely moved their village."

"Where?" Perry demanded.

With a shrug, Chapman answered, "Gone up or down the Salmon, I'd reckon. They whupped you already. Took what they wanted from your dead soldiers, then moved on."

"Surely Joseph has put out some war parties to roam this country, Colonel," Captain Joel G. Trimble asserted with an unmistakable air of superiority.

"At the least," added Second Lieutenant William Russell Parnell, "the chiefs assigned some spies to remain in the area to watch for us."

As some of the officers prattled on, Perry gazed into the canyon, not completely sure what he had spotted below. His eyes might be playing tricks on him the longer he stared. A dark clump here and there across that narrow ridgeline he had attempted to hold without a trumpet. More of them scattered back in this direction. Bodies. The unholy dead, their spirits raw and restless—

"Mr. Chapman." Perry suddenly turned on the civilian. "Select from your men a number of volunteers to accompany you for a brief reconnaissance."

The civilian cleared his throat, his eyes narrowing. "You ain't bringing these soldiers of yours down there with us?"

Perry straightened in the saddle, feeling every pair of eyes heatedly boring into him this warm midmorning. "No, Mr. Chapman. Make your search brief. Determine if there are any war parties left behind, then return to this position. We'll await your return."

For a moment Chapman glanced over the faces of the other citizens gathered from the nearby communities of Grangeville and Mount Idaho. Shearer, the Confederate major who, so it was said, had served on General Robert E. Lee's staff, shook his head. Eventually, Chapman wagged his head, too, his eyes boring into Perry's. "You ain't goin' down there with us, ain't no reason for me and my friends to stick our necks out neither."

"You won't search the valley?" Perry asked, his voice rising an octave.

"No, Commander. Not without what few soldiers you got left coming along with us, what soldiers can still fight if them Injuns show up again."

With a sigh of finality, Perry said, "I can't chance that, gentlemen. My battalion is diminished in strength as it is. I dare not lose any more—"

Almost as one, the civilians turned away behind Ad Chapman without uttering another word, starting back down the slope for Grangeville and Mount Idaho. A few of them peered over their shoulders at those relieved officers and soldiers nervously sitting there with their cavalry commander. Overlooking what had become a field of death.

Perry shuddered with the frustration he swallowed down, reined his horse around, and signaled with his arm for his battered, beaten battalion to follow him back to the settlements.

BY TELEGRAPH

An Indian War in Idaho.

IDAHO.

Official from General Howard.
WASHINGTON, June 20.— The following telegrams in
regard to the Indian troubles in Idaho were received
at the war department: From Gen. McDowell, San Francisco,
to Gen. Sherman, Washington.—The steamer California
arrived at Fort Townsend this morning with all the
troops from Alaska. I have ordered them to go to
Lewiston Friday morning. Gen. Hully will
go to Lewiston by that date.

[Signed] MCDOWELL, Major-Gen.

SAN FRANCISCO, June 19.—
General Sherman, Washington—
The following from General Howard at Laparoi to his staff
officer at department headquarters is just received.
There is rather gloomy news from the front by stragglers.
Captain Perry overtook the enemy, about 2,000 strong,
in a deep ravine well posted and was fighting there
when the last messenger left. I am expecting every
minute a messenger from him. The Indians are very
active and gradually increasing in strength, drawing
from other tribes. The movement indicates a combination
uniting nearly all the disaffected Indians and they
probably number 1,000 or 1,500 when united. Two
companies of infantry and twenty-five cavalry were
detached at Lewiston this morning and an order was
issued to every available man in the department,

> except at Forts Harney and Boize, to start all the
> troops at Harney or Boize except a small guard. They
> may receive orders en route turning them.

Dear Merciful God in heaven—did he feel all of his forty-six years at this moment.

Commander of the Military Department of the Columbia, headquartered at Portland, this veteran Civil War brigade leader, this survivor of the Apache wars in Arizona Territory, Brigadier General Oliver Otis Howard stepped into the midday light and onto the wide front porch of the joint Perry-FitzGerald residence here at Fort Lapwai, slapping some dust from his pale blue field britches with the gauntlet of the one leather glove he wore at the end of that one arm left him after the Civil War.

The ground of the wide parade yawning before him teemed with activity this Friday, the twenty-second of June, as company commanders and non-coms hustled their men into this final formation before they would dress left and depart for the seat of the Indian troubles. As the officers and enlisted were falling into ranks here at midday, the incessant dinging of the bell-mare as her mule string was brought into line, a little of the old thrill of war surged through him anew.

If ever Otis had hoped to be given one last chance to redeem himself after the shame unduly laid at his feet with the scandals at the Freedmen's Bureau down south . . . then Otis, as he had been called ever since childhood, would seize this golden opportunity to bring a swift and decisive end to this Nez Perce trouble. A foursquare and devout believer in the trials and the testing the Lord God would put only before those men destined for greatness, Howard was all the more certain that this was to be his moment.

The days ahead would yank him back from the precipice of obscurity, redeem him before Philip H. Sheridan and especially William Tecumseh Sherman himself—commander of this army—and win for Oliver Otis Howard a secure niche in the pantheon of our nation's heroes. This was right where he should have remained since losing his right arm in battle during Civil War. The winding, bumpy, unpredictable road that had seen him to this critical moment had been a journey that clearly prepared him for, and allowed him to recognize, this offered season of glory.

Born in the tiny farming village of Leeds along the Androscoggin River in the south of Maine on the eighth of November, 1830—the same day his maternal grandfather turned sixty-two—his mother dutifully named Oliver Otis for her father. His English ancestors had reached the shores of Massachusetts in 1643, migrating north to Leeds no more than a score of years before he was born.

After passing the most daunting entrance exams, he was admitted to the freshman class at Bowdoin College in September of 1846. Four years later found him beginning his career in the United State Army as a cadet underclassman at West Point. In the beginning he suffered some ostracism and ridicule because of his regular attendance of Bible classes, as well as his abolitionist views, being openly despised by no less than Custis Lee, the son of Colonel Robert E. Lee, who himself became superintendent of the acad-

emy in 1852. Nonetheless, one of Howard's fastest friends during his last two years at West Point proved to be Jeb Stuart, who would soon become the flower of the Confederate cavalry.

While Custis Lee was ranked first in their graduating class in June of '54, Howard was not far behind: proudly standing fourth in a field of forty-six. After those initial struggles, he was leaving the academy in success, a powerful esprit d'corps residing in his breast. Back when he had begun his term at the academy, Otis had little idea exactly what he wanted to become when he eventually graduated. But across those four intervening years, Oliver Otis Howard had become a soldier. It was the only profession he would ever know.

It had come as little surprise that the autumn of 1857 found him on the faculty of West Point, where he would remain until the outbreak of hostilities with the rebellious Southern states. Just prior to the bombardment and surrender of Fort Sumter, the spring of 1861 found Howard considering a leave of absence to attend the Bangor Theological Seminary. Until the opening of hostilities, the very notion that the North and South should ever go to war over their political squabbles was hardly worth entertaining.

But now it was war. Oliver Otis Howard had stepped forward to exercise his duty as a professional soldier. Rather than remaining as a lieutenant in the regular army, he instead lobbied for and won a colonelcy of the Third Maine Volunteers. Before that first year was out he had won his general's star, and scarcely a year later he became a major general.

Few men in the nation at that critical time had the training or experience to assume such lofty positions of leadership in either of those two great armies hurtling headlong into that long and bloody maelstrom. While Otis had indeed been an outstanding student during his time at the U. S. Military Academy, it was over the next four years that he, like many others, would struggle to learn his bloody profession on-the-job.

Ordered to lead his brigade of 3,000 toward the front in those opening days of war at the first Battle of Bull Run, on the way to the battlefield he and his men passed by the hundreds of General McDowell's wounded as they were hurried to the rear. The nearness of those whistling canisters of shot, the throaty reverberations of the cannon, the incessant rattle of small arms—not to mention the pitiful cries of the maimed, the sight of bloodied, limbless soldiers—suddenly gave even the zealous Howard pause.

He later wrote his dear Lizzie that there and then he put his fears in the hands of the Almighty, finding that in an instant his trepidation was lifted from him and the very real prospect of death no longer brought him any dread. From that moment on, Oliver Otis Howard would never again be anxious in battle.

Not long after George B. McClellan took over command of the Union Army, Howard was promoted to brigadier general of the Third Maine. In action during the Peninsula Campaign, his brigade found itself sharply engaged on the morning of the second day of the Battle of Fair Oaks as the Confederates launched a determined assault. Ordered to throw his remaining two regiments into the counterattack rather than holding them in reserve, Howard confidently stepped out in front of his men and gave the order to advance. Although Confederate minié balls were hissing through the brush and shredding the trees all around them, Howard continued to move among the front ranks of his men, conspicuous on horseback, leading his troops against the enemy's noisy advance.

When he was within thirty yards of that glittering line of bayonets and butternut gray uniforms, a lead .58-caliber bullet struck Otis in the right elbow. Somehow he remained oblivious to the pain as his men closed on the enemy. When they were just yards from engaging the Confederates in close-quarters combat, a bullet brought down his horse. As Howard was scrambling to his feet an instant later, a second ball shattered his right forearm just below the first wound.

With blood gushing from his flesh, Howard grew faint, stumbled, and collapsed, whereupon he turned over command of the brigade to another officer. Later that morning he was removed to a field hospital at the rear, where the surgeons explained the severity of his wounds, as well as the fact that there was little choice between gangrene—which would lead to a certain death—and amputation of the arm. By five o'clock that afternoon, the doctors went to work to save Howard's life.

Fair Oaks had been Otis's bravest hour.

Across these last few days, while panic spread like prairie fire across the countryside as word of the disaster at White Bird Canyon drifted in, townspeople, ranchers, and even the white missionaries from the nearby reservation had all streaked into Fort Lapwai, seeking the protection of its soldiers.

Now at last, five days after Perry's debacle on the White Bird, his army was ready to move into the fray. While he was leaving Captain William H. Boyle and his G Company of the Twenty-first U. S. Infantry to garrison this small post, Howard would now be at the head of two companies of the First U. S. Cavalry, one battery of the Fourth U. S. Artillery, and five companies of the Twenty-first—a total of 227 officers and men. One hundred of these were horse soldiers, and once Howard had reunited with Perry and his sixty-six survivors of White Bird Canyon, Otis would be leading a force of some three hundred after the Non-Treaty bands.

Oliver Otis Howard had a territory and civilians to protect and a bloody uprising to put down. To his way of thinking, he had just been handed what might well prove to be something far more than even his bravest hour had been at Fair Oaks.

This war with the Nez Perce could well be the defining moment of his entire life and military career.

CHAPTER TWO

—◄═◆═►—

JUNE 24, 1877

BY TELEGRAPH

———

Indian Outbreak in Idaho.

———

Desperate Engagement With
Serious Losses.

———

One Officer and Thirty-three
Men Killed.

———

The Salmon River Valley Desolated.

———

IDAHO.

———

Indian Outbreak.

SAN FRANCISCO, June 22.—A press dispatch from
Boise City confirms the report of the Indian outbreak
on the Salmon river. The Indians didn't kill women
and children, but allowed them to be taken under an
escort of friendly squaws to Slate creek, which has
thus far been left undisturbed. At Slate creek the
whites have fortified themselves in a stockade fort,
into which has been received the wives and children
of murdered men, with the families of men who escaped.
A large number of families, women and children, are
thus shut in in the midst of hostile Indians, without
adequate means of defense and, without aid, they will
certainly be overpowered and murdered. As the Indians
declare the determination to take the fort and murder
the men it can't be hoped that the Indians will again
spare the women and children after losses they must
sustain in capturing the fort, as the men will fight
to the last one. Our informant says he is reliably
informed that the Indians did not burn the buildings
or destroy property but cleaned out the country of
stock which they have driven to the south side of the

Salmon river where they seem to hope they will
ultimately be the undisturbed proprietors of all the
property the whites are now compelled to abandon.
They think, not without reason, that before the
country can be regained from them the army must be
created and a long and doubtful campaign passed
through. The Indians have now their camp and
headquarters on Salmon river, where the stock
stolen from the whites is gathered and pastured in
an extensive triangular-shaped region formed by
the Snake and Salmon rivers and a high mountain
range lying about the sources of Fayette and
Weaver rivers. Here there is abundant pasturage
for summer and winter, and there they will doubtless
make a final stand. In contradiction to previous
reports that troops behaved badly, our informant
says that by citizens, who were in the fight, he was
assured that the troops, although they allowed
themselves to be decoyed into ambush, displayed,
throughout the action, the utmost gallantry, and
fought like tigers. About twenty-five or thirty
soldiers were killed in about the same number of
minutes. The situation in northern Idaho far
exceeds in gravity any Indian outbreak of our day,
and it will tax the best resources of the government
and of the people immediately interested, to subdue
the Indians and restore peace to the country. The
Indians know that the army on this coast is but a
skeleton, and the people helpless for want of arms.
A special to the Portland Oregonian, just received
from Lewiston, June 21st, 8 a.m., says: Sixty-five
volunteers were to proceed from their defenses at Mount
Idaho to reconnoiter the position of the Indians, who
are supposed to be somewhere in the direction of the
Salmon river. A steamer arrived this forenoon, having
on board 107 troops. No extra arms came on the steamer.
About fifty volunteers have arrived here. A few of them
have no suitable arms, but are awaiting them from below.

ESS!" EMILY FITZGERALD CRIED IN EXASPERATION, WHIRLING ON HER
seven-year-old daughter. "Take your little brother and go outside
now while I am doing my best to finish this letter to your grand-
mother before the mail has to be posted."

"Yes, Mamma," responded young Elizabeth, immediately contrite at her
mother's sharp tone. She turned to her younger brother. "Come on, Bertie.
Let's find something to do outside with your toy horses until Mamma's done
with her letter."

With a sigh not in the least born of relief, but more so the sound one makes when faced with an arduous task, Emily fixed her eyes on the small cabinet photo of her mother she cradled in her left hand. How she wished that dear Quaker were there to comfort her at that moment.

Ever since he had returned to the fort from Portland, her husband, Jenkins —but better known as John—FitzGerald, the man whom she more often called Doctor, had hardly experienced a moment's rest, what with all the campaign preparations, all those duties laid about his shoulders now that General Howard had departed with his column to find the Nez Perce.

As she gazed at that sepia-toned memento of a visit to a Philadelphia photographer's studio with her mother, Emily angrily scolded herself for being so selfish, then propped the photograph beside the letter she was crafting.

Why wasn't she able to just accept how much better it was that Howard had decided to leave her husband behind at Fort Lapwai to see to supply-train and organizational matters for the time being? Far better than watching him ride off with the others that might not return! Dr. Jenkins A. Fitz-Gerald, army surgeon, First U. S. Cavalry. A man of duty and honor . . .

In all their years together since the Civil War, she hadn't addressed him as Jenkins more than two, perhaps three, times. Instead, she called him John or—mostly—Doctor.

He had been away from the post, visiting Portland on army business, when news of the murders first reached Fort Lapwai. How glad she had been that her John hadn't been here when Colonel Perry marched off with his hundred men. There simply was no convincing Emily that John wouldn't have been among all those dead left to rot on the White Bird battle-field.

But when he did get back upriver, what a homecoming that had been! Even though they both knew it wasn't for long. General Howard was gathering 227 men, a complement of eight companies, from nearby posts and tiny garrisons: two troops of cavalry, five companies of infantry, along with a company of artillery who were armed with two Gatling guns and a mountain howitzer. My, but how they would go to work on Joseph's murderers now!

> *Fort Lapwai*
> *June 24, 1877*

Dear Mamma,

> *I have not been able to write or even to think for a week. Such a confusion as our quiet little Lapwai has been in. When I can, I will write the particulars. Since the battle, we have all had a great deal to occupy us. Mrs. Boyle and I have been with Mrs. Theller . . . Then all week there have been troops passing through and we have entertained the officers . . . The parade ground is full of horses, the porches are full of trunks and blankets, everybody is rushing about, and everything is in confusion. My brain is in as much confusion as anything else. The army is so reduced, and none of the companies are full, and all the troops that can possibly be*

*gathered from all this region only amount to three hundred. Those
are now in the field, and it is a little handful! Oh, the government,
I hate it! Much it respects and cares for the soldier who, at a
moment's notice, leaves his family and sacrifices his life for some
mistaken Indian policy . . . I wish we were well out of it. The Nez
Perce Indians are at war with the Whites. What a blow to the
theories of Indian civilization. The whole tribe is wavering, and
we don't know when it will all end—*

"Excuse me, Mrs. FitzGerald."

Emily turned with a start, finding the slight woman framed by the open
doorway leading onto the front porch, her pale hands clutched before her
swollen belly like a pair of white doves that might take flight if she were not
mindful of them. And those red, red eyes.

"Yes, Alice."

The very-much pregnant Alice Hurlburt cleared her throat, took one step
closer to the surgeon's wife, then said, "If it's fine by you, ma'am . . . can my
young'uns play with your li'l ones?"

"I just sent Bessie outside with Bert."

"Yes, I saw," Mrs. Hurlburt replied, half-turning her head out the door,
then back again. "They all play so well together."

"It will be fine, Alice. Yes, quite fine."

Those red-rimmed, cried-out eyes did their best to smile at Emily as Alice
Hurlburt turned back through the open doorway, stepping into the shade of
the porch, little protection from the growing heat of that summer afternoon.

Emily FitzGerald swatted at a fly, dipped her pen into the inkwell, and
continued writing.

*I have a sad, sad story to tell about the family of one of those who
did not come home after Joseph's murderers ambushed Colonel
Perry's men. It appears that William Hurlburt made a fine mess
of his life as a civilian. Problem was, he had a wife and two
children. With nowhere else to turn, and no other way to feed his
family, Mr. Hurlburt joined the army and soon found himself
transferred to Nez Perce country. Only recently did his wife and
children come west to join him at Lapwai. In such hardship
cases with enlisted men, the government will pay the costs of
transportation of a man's family to his duty station, but a little
is deducted from every paycheck until those costs are paid off.*

*And now it's clear to see she is with child again, Mamma.
Pitiful creature, poor Alice is, for she lost her husband to the Nez
Perce last week on White Bird Creek. Now she finds herself
without a husband, deeply in debt, and without any prospects on
how to return east to her people. Not knowing what else to do, I
performed on my Christian charity and took them in until their
situation can be sorted through. She is a very nice little woman,
and her children are as nice as I know. It does my heart good to
have them under our roof instead of being left out in the cold now*

that the army will no longer provide for her, but comes demanding repayment on its transportation debt. The children play so well together.

She is left destitute. After her sickness,* we will all help her. A purse will be raised to take her back to her friends. She is a helpless sort of a little woman, and I never saw such a look of distress in my life as has taken possession of her face.

Outside, the children were shrieking with abandon and glee as they chased one another across the grass of the nearby parade. Emily went to the window, pushed aside the gauzy curtain, and peered into the unblemished June sunshine. *It is a blessing,* she thought, *a blessing the children can play as if they haven't a care in the world. As if one father isn't dead, mortifying in this harsh sun on an abandoned battlefield, and the other father soon to be marching off with those who will make the Nez Perce pay for their bloody crimes.*

Search as she may out the window, Emily didn't catch a glimpse of the Doctor. So she returned to her letter, settling into the ladder-back chair at the small secretary once more, then dipped her pen into the inkwell.

Soon enough their parting would come. In a war the soldiers needed their surgeons. All too soon Howard would summon John to the battlefront. Like other officers, dutiful and honor-bound, he would kiss his family farewell, mount up, and ride off to join the others.

She dragged the back of her left hand across both damp cheeks and continued writing.

This last week has been the most dreadful I have ever passed through. John came home, and I felt a little relieved of the horrors that hung over me when I heard he was not to go out with the first detachment. I heard General Howard say, when arranging his orders, that someone must, for the present, be left here to arrange supplies, medicines, etc., and Doctor had better be left here, as he belongs to the post . . . You can't imagine how sad it all is here. Here are these nice fellows gathered around our table, all discussing the situation and all knowing they will never all come back.

One leaves his watch and little fixings and says, "If one of those bullets gets me, send this to my wife." Another gave me his boy's photograph to keep for him, as he could not take it. He kept his wife's with him, and twice he came back to look at the boy's before he started off. One officer left a sick child, very ill; another left a wife to be confined next month. What thanks do they all get for it? No pay, and abuse from the country that they risk their lives to protect . . .

Your loving daughter,
Emily F.

---

*That peculiar nineteenth-century euphemism for pregnancy.

P. S. If John had been here, he would have gone with Colonel Perry and, in all probability, been killed. I am so thankful of that trip to Portland and hope and pray God will watch over the Doctor as wisely through all this horrible war. Even if he goes away from Lapwai, I shall be glad I am here, for we can hear from the troops in a few hours. We do hope this next fight will decide the matter forever.

Em.

CHAPTER THREE

---◆◆◆---

JUNE 24, 1877

BY TELEGRAPH

The Idaho Indian Troubles.

Attempted General Combination of all the Tribes.

IDAHO.

Latest from the Scene of Indian Disturbances.
BOISE CITY, June 23.—Hon. T. E. Logan, mayor of
Boise City, and Bonin Costin, member of the legislative
council, who left here on Wednesday for the purpose of
visiting the Indians encamped on Great Camas prairie,
twenty-five miles southeast of this place, returned
at noon, accompanied by fourteen of the chiefs of the
Indians there assembled. There are now encamped in
that locality about 1,500 Indians of both sexes and
all ages, embracing members of Bannacks, Shoshones
and Yellowstone tribes. Logan and Costin went to
Willow creek, forty miles distant, where they found
a party of Indians. They made known their object,
to obtain the disposition of the Indians and their
intentions. The Indians were asked to send forward
their best riders to the main camp, and request the
principal chief to meet the commission at Willow
creek. The Indians complied and soon the chiefs
made their appearance and an interview took place
which revealed the fact that these Indians had been
visited by emissaries from the Nez Perces and other
hostiles in the north, and a portion of them had
been considering whether to remain friendly to
the whites or to join the hostiles . . .

SAN FRANCISCO, June 23.—A Portland press dispatch
says General Howard telegraphs from Fort Laparoi, June

21st: Captain Miller with 300 men leaves for the front
this evening. The Indian prisoners state that the
soldiers left wounded on the field were killed but
not mutilated. A steamer arrived at Lewiston this morning
with 125 troops and a large quantity of arms, etc.

APTAIN DAVID PERRY WASN'T SURE IF HE READ DISAPPROVAL IN GENERAL
Howard's eyes . . . or merely a deep, deep disappointment.
"Is that the extent of your report, Colonel?" Howard used Perry's
brevet rank.

The captain cleared his throat nervously. "Not exactly, sir. With your permission—"

"There's more?"

"Not really any more to my report, General," then Perry felt angry with himself for hemming and hawing. "Yes, sir. I've have something to say."

Howard shifted uneasily on the camp stool in front of his headquarters tent pitched near the base of one of the low hills here at the army's camp surrounding the Norton ranch on Cottonwood Creek.

Back in those early days of this dirty little outbreak, Benjamin Norton and his family had been flushed from their home by renegade warriors, chased onto the Camas Prairie, and run down miles from succor or aid. While Norton and others in the same party had died of their bullet wounds, his wife, son, and niece had survived their hellish ordeal. Now the road ranch stood in shambles: Warriors had ransacked the house as they rummaged through the white family's possessions, everything not taken or burned lay about in utter disorder, clothing cut or torn apart, drawers yanked out and dumped over, chairs chopped into kindling, sacks of sugar and salt strewn across the wood floors, an unrestrained victory riot gone completely mad.

The only signs that this had once been a peaceful setting might well have been the upturned milking pails still resting on their corral fenceposts, a few unfed chickens scratching in the yard, and a lonely pup that cowered in the shadows beneath the porch.

Arriving here yesterday, the twenty-third, at noon after a forty-three-mile march from Lapwai, the general had put his men into bivouac, intending to use this spot as his base of operations against the Non-Treaty Nez Perce who were surely still ravaging the surrounding countryside. While Howard's eight companies established their perimeter, dug rifles pits, and organized a horse-guard, the general sent word to the nearby settlements of Grangeville and Mount Idaho with orders for Captain David Perry to report to his commanding officer at Cottonwood Station.

Taking the better part of two hours on the morning of the twenty-fourth, Perry had detailed every step of his march from Fort Lapwai, his approach to the seat of the troubles, along with a studied emphasis on the testimony of the local civilians that the Indians were sure to flee, certain to throw down their arms without a fight at the first sign of the soldiers, that Perry was convinced he must act quickly before the thieves escaped across the Salmon with their stolen horses and cattle.

At that point the captain explained his march across the White Bird divide, awaiting dawn when they could march down into the canyon for the attack.

"You had all your men deployed before they began falling back?" Howard had asked more than once.

"Yes, sir."

"With none of your elements held in reserve?"

"No, General."

Howard brooded at that. "But you chose to place the civilians on your far left, at a critical place along your line."

"Yes, I did."

"And that's where the Nez Perce rolled up your line, beginning with those untrained civilians."

The captain reluctantly nodded. "That appears to be exactly what happened."

It was a painful two hours—some of the hardest Perry had ever endured in the army. But these next few minutes, and what more he had to tell General O. O. Howard, might well be the most painful of all, or this might be just what saved his hash in this man's army.

"Well, Colonel," Howard said wearily as he tossed out the cold dregs from his tin coffee cup. "You said you had one thing more to report."

"I have a concern as to Major Trimble." He spoke in little above a harsh whisper, his heart thumping in his chest as he struggled to control his anger, an anger at the mere mention of the man's name.

Captain Joel G. Trimble, brevet major, commander of H Company, First U. S. Cavalry—and Perry's subordinate at Fort Lapwai—had ridden into the valley of the White Bird with David Perry . . . but had been the first to race back out in the retreat.

"Trimble failed to acknowledge your orders for him to halt and assist in your orderly retreat?" Howard asked, dumbfounded.

"Lieutenant Parnell will back me up, General," Perry asserted. "We both saw Major Trimble stop at the top of the divide, turn, and look back down at us as we closed the file. He had to have seen us calling for his assistance, seen us waving him back to cover our retreat."

"What did the major do?"

"We watched him turn away and disappear at the top," the captain explained. "I didn't see him again until I reached the Grangeville settlement—"

"Have you confronted Trimble with your accusations?"

Perry could no longer peer into Howard's eyes. He dropped his gaze to the thick grass beneath his boots. "More times than I care to count, sir—I've asked myself why I didn't upbraid him there and then."

Howard clinked down the empty coffee cup and asked, "You didn't state your charges against him?"

Still unable to look the general in the eye, Perry said, "No. The only reason I have been able to figure out for my failure to demand an explanation of him is that I found myself barely able to throttle back my anger whenever I'm around Trimble. I'm certain that if I ever got started on this topic in his presence, I might not be responsible for my actions—"

"Are you charging him with insubordination?"

It took a few moments before the captain finally raised his eyes to look at Howard's face, then nodded. "Yes, General."

"And dereliction of duty?"

"That too, yes, sir. In my opinion, the battle was lost when his left side of the line disintegrated. He could have held—even after the civilians were rolled up. But within minutes he had abandoned me. Major Trimble abandoned everyone who was behind him in the retreat."

"How many men was that, Colonel?"

Perry straightened and brought his shoulders out. "I doubt there was any more than a handful of soldiers in front of Trimble in their retreat out of the canyon."

Howard wagged his head and stared into the fire. "He was out ahead of all the rest?"

"Yes, sir."

"These . . . are serious charges." For a long time Howard continued to stare at the nearby fire. When he finally spoke, it was to call out to his dog-robber, who was perched on a canvas stool just out of earshot from that quiet discussion the two officers had been having. "Orderly, pour me some more coffee."

Perry watched the young private hurry over and drag the coffeepot off the coals with a greasy towel. These orderlies, who worked as servants for their superior officers, had been given that appellation commonly used by the army of that day: *dog-robber.* With the coffee poured and handed to the general, the private again retreated out of hearing.

"Colonel Perry," Howard sighed with finality. "We've got a war exploding around us at this moment."

"Sir?"

Howard took a long sip of the coffee, then continued without looking across at the captain. "For the moment, I don't dare sacrifice a single one of my officers through disciplinary action."

That stunning admission caught Perry by surprise. "B-But, General. I wasn't considering bringing Major Trimble up on charges. No disciplinary action. Perhaps an official reprimand from you was all that I could expect. If his offense goes without notice, it serves to show a bad example to the enlisted men who all witnessed his dereliction—"

"Colonel," Howard interrupted him. "For me to take any action against the major would be to relieve him of duty, sending him back to Fort Lapwai under escort until an official inquiry is made, and I determine if a court should be called. I'd be taken up with having to prefer charges and you taken up along with me. We simply don't have the time for that right now. Instead, we've got a war to fight."

Perry kept staring at Howard's bearded face, wondering when the general would look up from his coffee tin, when Howard would take his eyes off that smoky fire. While he hadn't graduated near the top of his class, David Perry was nonetheless slowly realizing that he had this situation sorted out for what it was. There would be no arguing with the general's decision.

"Very good, sir," he said with a somber note of regret. "I understand this matter of preferring charges against Major Trimble will only be delayed for the time being?"

"Yes, by all means. Just for the time being."

He dragged his heels together, straightened, and saluted his commanding officer. "Very good, General. For the time being. . . . After all, we do have a war to fight."

> *Fort Lapwai*
> *June 25, 1877*

> *Dear Aunt Annie,*

> *Your nice letter came this morning and decided me to write to you.*
> *You ask about the Indians. They are devils, and I will not feel easy again until we are safely out of the country they claim as theirs. Joseph's Non-Treaty band was given thirty days to come onto the reservation. On the last day of the thirty, when everybody was comfortably settled and never dreaming of trouble, they began to murder the settlers.*
> *Doctor was away in Portland. He came hurrying home horrified. He had heard this post was burned and all sorts of alarming rumors. I felt all my calmness and bravery departing when he came home, as he only came in the morning and expected to move out with the troops in the evening, but the General found it necessary to leave someone to forward supplies and look after the troops that are passing through here and left Dr. F. for the present. Dr. Alexander . . . is the chief medical officer in the field. Dr. Sternberg . . . was also with us last week and has moved on to the front. We have been busy entertaining the officers who are passing through, with our hearts aching, knowing they will never all come back, and fearing, too, all the time, an attack on the post.*
> *We had one horrible false alarm of an Indian attack last week. The long roll was sounded, the men were all under arms, and the women and children all gathered into one house around which there are breastworks . . . Poor Mrs. Theller joined Mrs. Boyle and me. She had strapped on her dead husband's cartridge belt and was carrying his carbine and looked every bit as if she were ready to avenge her husband's brutal murder.*
> *We fear there will be a horrible battle within the next few days. Everybody here is busy day and night. My poor John! I have not had five minutes to talk with him since he came home . . .*
> *Doctor wanted to send us right home, but I can't leave him or leave here, even when he goes to join the troops that are in the front, as I can hear of him so often and so immediately here. If I should lose him (I hope and pray he will be spared to me) I would, of course, come right home to you all and expect you to take care of me, at least until I could think what I could do with my helpless little babies . . . Doctor says he thinks us safe here, or he would not let us stay. We are all well, only nearly worn out by the excitement and constant strain. I start at every unusual sound*

and feel the strength departing from my knees and elbows. John declares I have lost ten pounds. Everybody feels blue and anxious for the result. Another victory for Joseph would bring to his standard all the disaffected Indians in the Department, and the whole Nez Perces tribe is wavering.

After Lunch

The Nez Perce Agent lunched with us. He says he learns from friendly Indians that Joseph's command is not a large one, does not number much over a hundred, but that hundred is prepared to fight to the death. The Indians say they know they will be hung if taken, and they mean to kill as many soldiers as they can first and then die themselves. Our officers going through here think the campaign will be a short but severe one. I wish all the Indians in the country were at the bottom of the Red Sea. I suppose the country will have trouble until they are exterminated.

Your affectionate niece,
Emily FitzGerald

CHAPTER FOUR

JUNE 25, 1877

BY TELEGRAPH

Great Storm in the West.

Extending Over a Large Portion of
the West.

OMAHA, June 25.—The storm, very general
throughout the west, was first heard of at Cheyenne
yesterday evening. Heavy hail and wind extended north
of Sioux City, south of Kansas City, and
over the state of Iowa.

FROM THE EDGE OF THE TREE LINE, FIRST SERGEANT MICHAEL MC-Carthy turned in his saddle and looked back at the Camas Prairie laid out behind them like a soggy, rumpled bedcloth. Their bivouac on Cottonwood Creek was back there some fourteen miles or so through the sheets of sleety rain and wet snow.

H Company had followed Captain Joel G. Trimble and a Nez Perce tracker away from the Nortons' road ranch an hour after sunrise that morning, the twenty-fifth of June. While the general himself would be coming along at a much slower pace this Monday, Howard had ordered Trimble and his men to make a reconnaissance in force toward Slate Creek and relieve the citizens under seige at the settlement. In addition, Company H should be prepared to turn the Nez Perce when Howard's column flushed the enemy from their Salmon River hiding places.

With that last look over his shoulder, McCarthy still couldn't spot any signs of the general's column moving away from Cottonwood in the dance of those intermittent but heavy and wet snowflakes. Plans were that the rest of Howard's men would march for Grangeville and Mount Idaho, halting briefly to reassure the frightened settlers taking refuge there. Then the column would push on over the divide for Perry's battlefield, where they would bury the dead before pursuing the Non-Treaty bands up the Salmon. That should give Trimble's H enough time to be in position at the Slate Creek barricades, where they could stem the red tide Howard's column was sure to stir into motion.

"Sounds to me we got the darty duty again, Major," McCarthy had growled to Second Lieutenant William R. Parnell earlier that morning as they were forming up their company, using the officer's brevet rank.

The tall and fleshy fellow Irishman's eyes darted over the ten new men who had arrived at Cottonwood two days before behind Second Lieutenant Thomas T. Knox, on detached duty from Fort Walla Walla. "Not all the luftenant's men are proper sojers, Sergeant dear," he replied guardedly.

"Must've picked up them recruits down at Walla Walla," McCarthy assessed the newcomers. "Them weeds look green as grass."

Parnell nodded. "But we'll take them shavetail boyos because you and me need 'em so bad. Ain't that right, Sergeant?"

True enough: Lieutenant Knox and his ten recruits bolstered the company roster at a most crucial time. Eleven men would go far to replacing the thirteen dead and one wounded ripped from the rolls of H Company on the seventeenth of June at White Bird. Their recent arrival brought Trimble's command up to some thirty men. Not a full company, but a damn sight better than a puny scouting patrol now that they were riding off against the red hellions who had butchered so many of McCarthy's friends eight days before.

Still, to get to Slate Creek, Trimble's men had to make sure they avoided any roving war parties and gave the Non-Treaty bands a wide berth. To accomplish that, H Company would take a circuitous route, following an abandoned and little-used trail through the high country to reach the mining camp of Florence. From there they would double back several miles, staying behind the ridges, angling down to reach the civilians who had gathered behind their barricades on the east side of the Salmon, at the mouth of Slate Creek.

There . . . in the distance, for a brief moment before he could no longer see the Camas Prairie laid out beneath the low-slung clouds, Sergeant McCarthy thought he saw the first dark figures snaking onto the grassy, rolling plains. Emerging from Cottonwood Station, as the locals called Norton's road ranch.

He turned around and settled himself miserably into that damp McClellan saddle again. It made him feel a little better diving into these forested hills and the unknown, realizing that Howard's column actually would be somewhere at their rear.

It was for sure that Colonel Perry was no fighting man. By the same token, neither was McCarthy's own company commander, Captain Trimble. He, even before the colonel, had turned tail and scampered away when things got warm. So it sure as hell didn't give a man a secure feeling to go traipsing off behind a man who had shown the white feather to those red heathens.

McCarthy quickly shot another glance at Knox's ten new recruits up from Walla Walla. Then his eyes continued down the column to those battle-weary survivors of the White Bird fray. And finally to the broad back of that fleshy Irishman, Parnell.

If the red buggers jumped H Company somewhere in these hills, at least the two of them would manage to hurl profane Irish curses at the red buggers until they got down to their last bullet. The one a man always saved for himself.

OLIVER OTIS HOWARD was more than startled.

He had been shaken to his core to look over the men of Perry's command who had remained behind at the settlements while the captain rode to meet Howard at Cottonwood.

How different they are in numbers, different in their appearance, not the brisk and hearty troopers that left Fort Lapwai the week previous, he thought as his horse slowly moved toward the barricades.

Now the look on their faces, the studied horror in their eyes, reminded him of the war-weary, frightened soldiers he had seen every day, every campaign, in their war against the rebellious Southern states. Although those survivors of the White Bird fight cheered the general's arrival with the rest of the cavalry now placed under Perry's command, Howard realized those survivors had nonetheless been changed for all time.

At a parting of the roads on the outskirts of Grangeville, Howard had sent his infantry—B, D, E, H, and I Companies of the Twenty-first, as well as E Company of the Fourth Artillery—on ahead, with orders to make camp at Johnson's ranch near the base of the White Bird divide. The general would continue on with Captain David Perry, who was now leading a new battalion of horse soldiers: E and L Companies of the First U. S. Cavalry companies.

After an hour's layover in tiny Grangeville, during which time he gathered intelligence on the Non-Treaty bands from the locals and inspected those supplies, J. W. "John" Crooks was making available to the column, Howard resumed his march for Mount Idaho. With cheering, exuberant citizens swarming around him in that neighboring community, the general examined the hastily built fortress with former British officer H. W. Croasdaile before he walked down the main street to reach Loyal P. Brown's Mount Idaho House.

"Quiet! Quiet!" Brown shouted above the noisy throng of more than 250 settlers, ranchers, and soldiers, too. "I've prevailed upon General Howard to say a few words before he rejoins his column at Johnson's ranch. Ladies and gentlemen—I give you the man who will right the wrongs done us. The man who will recapture our stock and property from the red thieves. The man who will quickly put down this uprising and punish the Nez Perce. . . . I give you General Howard!"

He couldn't remember when he had been given such a splendid ovation. Surely not since those days of the Freedmen's Bureau, before the scandals, before he was forever tainted with the vicious slander that had almost ruined his career, almost ruined the work of a lifetime. How that raucous applause and hearty huzzahs thundered in his ears and refreshed his flagging spirit here as he set about snuffing out the first flames of a territory-wide war.

But as he self-consciously cleared his throat, Otis promised himself he would make it a short speech. Just the way he was going to make this a short war. "Ladies and gentlemen. Friends, and fellow countrymen. We have now taken the field in good earnest. More troops are on the way to join us."

That declaration elicited another noisy round of applause before he was allowed to continue.

"I propose to take prompt measures for the pursuit and punishment of the hostile Indians, and wish you—each and every one of you—to help me in that endeavor. Help me in the way of information and supplies, as much does lie in your power."

A quiet smattering of applause began what quickly exploded into a noisy response from the approving throng, more than two hundred heads bobbing in agreement with his proposal. Otis stood there, letting the praise wash over him a moment, sensing the strength it gave him, how it seeped into every muscle to give might to his own efforts in the coming struggle.

When the crowd settled, he said in a quieter tone, "I sympathize deeply with you in the loss of life, and in the outrages to which your families have been subjected. Rest assured that no stone will be left unturned to give you redress, to give you protection in the future."

An instant applause erupted again, and Otis stepped back, gesturing to L. P. Brown. The hotel owner came forward and said a few final words before the two of them turned to join Sarah Brown at the open doorway. As the general's party stopped just inside the Browns' hotel, a young man in his late twenties hurried forward, rolling a sleeve down over his bare forearm.

"General Howard," Brown began, "I'd like you to meet Dr. John Morris. Mount Idaho's physician."

They clumsily shook left hands and Otis said, "You're caring for the wounded, Doctor?"

The Missouri-born Morris nodded. "I was visiting Portland when news of the outbreak reached us. Boarded the next steamer for Lewiston and made my way over from there."

"How long have you been practicing in this area?"

"Came to Mount Idaho in seventy-five," the doctor explained. "Not long after I earned my license to practice from St. Louis Medical College."

Brown stepped up. "Dr. Morris returned home three days ago, the twenty-second. Poor fella hasn't had much sleep since."

"I catch a nap when and where I can, General," Morris explained.

Howard looked into the young man's warm eyes. "May I see, may I talk to the people, the civilians you are caring for?"

"Of course. By all means," Morris replied and started away.

In several of the small rooms on that floor, and on the second story as well, Morris led Howard and Brown to the bedside of every victim of the Nez Perce terror. Many sobbed quietly as the old one-armed soldier moved among their beds, cots, or simple pallets spread upon the floor.

Howard turned to the hotel owner. "Mr. Brown, what about the man you started for Fort Lapwai with news of the murders?"

Brown shook his head. "Lew Day? He isn't here anymore."

Howard turned to the physician, asking, "No longer under your care, Dr. Morris?"

"By the time I arrived here from Portland, his leg wound was in a dreadful condition," Morris declared. "I explained to Lew that it was his leg or his life. He agreed to the amputation." Then the physician sighed. "But I think he was so drained of all strength that he simply didn't survive for long after I took his leg."

"He died?"

Brown said, "We buried Lew Day up in the Masonic cemetery."

"Please, take me to the others," Howard stated, gesturing with his left arm. "I want to see all the others who suffered these attacks and outrages."

Joe Moore was barely able to speak, weakened so from a great loss of blood, critically wounded in the attack on the Norton wagon on the Camas Prairie.*

Both Herman Faxon and Theodore Swarts were still recovering from their terrible wounds suffered in the battle in White Bird Canyon. Jennie Norton lay in a small room, watched over and cared for by her son, Hill, and her younger sister, Lynn Bowers.

Next door lay the wounded Mrs. Chamberlin, who had watched the Nez Perce butcher her husband, murder one of her daughters, then suffered repeated assault by the members of the war party who had jumped the Norton party on the Camas Prairie road.

"She's suffered . . . unspeakable horror," Dr. Morris explained in a whisper at Howard's ear as the general stood gazing at the woman. "Every outrage they could have committed, the Indians perpetrated on her. Took her husband, one of her children, too. Then they repeatedly shamed her."

Howard's eyes drifted now to the youngster playing quietly on the floor with a tiny wooden horse, perfectly content near the end of the bed. "Whose child?"

"Mrs. Chamberlin's," Sarah Brown declared. "Unable to speak. The savages cut its poor tongue off."

"Never talk again?" Howard asked in a whisper as he started toward the side of the bed. There he bent slightly, laid his hand on Mrs. Chamberlin's, and closed his eyes in silent prayer.

When he concluded, Howard straightened and stared down a moment into the toddler's big brown eyes before he turned away with the doctor.

Besides Williams George, H. C. "Hurdy Gurdy" Brown, and Albert Benson, Morris was also tending the wounds of little Maggie Manuel.

"She tells us Joseph killed her mother and baby brother," L. P. Brown declared in a soft voice at the doorway to another room as Howard looked in on the child sleeping upon a pallet made of blankets folded upon the floor.

"How does she know it was Joseph?" Howard asked.

Brown shrugged. "Says she's seen him before."

"But Maggie's grandfather and an Irish miner never found the bodies, General," Morris asserted.

Howard asked, "She broke her arm?"

"The Irishman I mentioned—he set her arm before beginning their journey here," Morris said. "A good job of it, too. Didn't have to rebreak it at all. Farther up that same arm, she had suffered a penetrating injury—an arrow the miner managed to remove. We're watching that closely for infection.

---

*Cries from the Earth, vol. 14, the Plainsmen series.

Keeping the wound open and treated with sulphur. She's been brave through it all—knowing as she does that she's lost both her parents to the Indians."

"Merciful God in Heaven," Howard whispered as he turned away, unable to look upon the child anymore. Feeling as if he could never gaze upon another wounded youngster as long as he lived. Beneath his full beard, the general felt the blood drain from his skin, his face blanch.

War was for men. Not for these women and their babies. War was a profession to be practiced by men, practiced on other men. Not on these innocent victims of such barbaric cruelty.

"I've seen enough, Doctor," he said in a soft voice, sensing the sweat bead on his brow as he replaced the hat upon his head, his flesh grown clammy. "I think . . . I've seen quite enough."

CHAPTER FIVE

June 25–26, 1877

HO GOES THERE?"

The instant that harsh voice challenged them out of the inky night, Sergeant Michael McCarthy snapped awake in the saddle.

Their company commander was the first to reply as the thirty-some soldiers of H Company and a handful of hangers-on from Mount Idaho clattered to a noisy halt in the dark, just after 2:00 A.M. on that Monday morning, 25 June. "Major Joel Trimble—First U. S. Cavalry!"

"Cavalry!" a second, different voice shouted now, less threatening and an octave higher with relief and celebration.

There came a sudden bustle of noise from the darkness in their front: sounds of shuffling, running feet, several more muffled voices mixed with a little unrestrained exuberance as the wooded river bottom came alive.

"Open this goddamned gate!" a new voice was raised. "Get it open for them soldiers!"

"By bloody damn," Lieutenant Parnell exclaimed with no small measure of exhaustion beside McCarthy, "appears we've found the settlers of Slate Creek!"

Just past two-thirty, early on the morning of 26 June, Company H had done just that.

It had been closing in on complete darkness the night before when they reached the tiny mining settlement of Florence, finally coaxing out a few of the Chinese and what few whites still remained in the town to report what they knew of the marauding Indians. It was useless attempting to pry any information from the Oriental laborers, but two of the white miners had a little news to relay on the movements of the Non-Treaty Bands. The Nez Perce were no longer encamped at the mouth of the White Bird. They had eased south, up the Salmon toward Horseshoe Bend.

"The savages appear to be acting as if we won't attack 'em again," Trimble had explained to the entire company just before he ordered them to remount.

Parnell had asked, "We still going on to Slate Creek, Major?"

"Get them saddled, Sergeant McCarthy," was Trimble's only reply as he ignored his lieutenant. "We're not sticking around here when we've got ground to cover."

Those weary, saddle-galled troopers had climbed back into their McClellans after no more than fifteen minutes with their boots on the ground and pushed on. Twelve miles later, as McCarthy's watch was nearing midnight, Trimble called for another halt in an open patch of meadow surrounded by stands of timber. The moon was just then tearing itself off the horizon to the east, somewhere behind the Bitterroot Mountains.

"Don't loosen your cinches, boyos," McCarthy warned his men. "You can eat your tacks if you got 'em, but no pipes. Remember what happened at the White Bird. No god-blame-it pipes in this country."

After something less than an hour Trimble gave the order to remount and they marched on, encountering some crusted snow just after leaving the small meadow and climbed ever higher. What with those snowfields reflecting the dim starlight, the whole countryside limned by a bright, silvery half-moon, the view was stunning. In awe at such breathtaking scenery, McCarthy knew it would take a pen much more eloquent than his to do justice to their cross-country ride.

The quiet of that mountain wilderness, the blackness of the night that surrounded them, the rhythmic plodding of the saddle horse beneath him—all of it proved more than McCarthy could fight. He drifted off and was dozing in the saddle when those voices called out from the dark.

After a brief celebration and a shaking of hands all around, the settlers helped Trimble's men find a corral for their weary horses, then led the soldiers within their log walls. Clutching their blankets about their shoulders, the troopers collapsed here or there, wherever a man might find enough room to stretch out, close his eyes, and sink immediately into a well-earned sleep.

By the gray light of false dawn McCarthy came awake, rolling out to join two civilians at the west wall where they had a low fire going, coffee warmed to see them through their watch.

"William Watson's the name," the older man introduced himself with a big hand.

The sergeant replied, "I heard you're the one knowed how to build this fort."

"That's right. Got all my learning during the war," Watson explained.

"Your education come in handy here," McCarthy said, admiring the sturdiness of the timbers the men had sunk into three-foot-deep trenches, then back-filled. "Can't see how the bloody h'athens could've broke in here on you."

Norman Gould said, "Bill here, he saw to it we'd get all the women and young'un into the stone house back yonder if the bastards broke over the walls."

"We made the house our powder magazine," Watson explained, jabbing a thumb toward the structure. "Blow up everything—everyone, too—before the Nez Perce got their hands on 'em."

"Didn't know how long we'd have to hold out," George Greer said. "Word was that General Howard was somewhere in the field, but we didn't know just where you soldiers was, or when you'd get here to us."

"Wasn't the general moved out first," McCarthy explained dolefully. "Maybe it had been Howard what led us down into White Bird 'stead of Colonel Perry his cowardly self there'd be more of me friends alive to greet this very morning."

The coffee was good, but the sun that broke over the hills that morning felt even better. Trimble had McCarthy tell the men that H Company would be spending a day of rest at Slate Creek—recruiting their horses and gathering strength for the rest of their mission.

Later that Tuesday morning, some of the women and children ventured from the stone house, stepping outside the safety of the stockade walls for the first time in more than a week of dread. While the rest of the women were grateful for, and the children excited about, the arrival of the soldiers, not one of Trimble's cavalrymen got a peek at either Helen Walsh or Elizabeth Osborn.

"Rumor has it they was violated," Parnell explained in a whisper as he and McCarthy walked up the slope to relieve two men of their watch along the Salmon.

"Raped?"

"Shhh!" Parnell rasped angrily. "It's talk like that made them two women fear to show their faces."

"They was . . . shamed by the h'athens?"

The lieutenant nodded as they neared the improvised rifle pits. "Both of 'em, over and over again by the red bastards. 'Cause of it, neither of them women gonna ever be the same again."

It made his blood boil, to think of those painted up, blood-splattered, stink-smeared warriors humiliating, dishonoring, shaming those two women.

The sergeant turned to stare a long moment down at the stone house, his heart breaking for both victims of such unspeakable horror. "No small wonder is it? Why them poor women can't hardly face their friends no more."

"They lost their husbands, too, I heard," Parnell said. "Come out of it only with their wee ones."

"Them's the ones we're fighting the Nez Perce for, Lieutenant Parnell," McCarthy growled. "Them women and children. They're the reason I wanna kill me ever' last Injun buck I can put in my sights, or get my hands around. They're less'n human, ever' last bloody one of 'em."

WE SHOULD REACH the scene before midmorning, General," declared Captain David Perry after he had saluted the campaign's commander in the misty damps of predawn that twenty-sixth day of June.

"You understand my purpose in going into that valley is not to engage the Nez Perce," Howard reminded.

"You explained that to me last night."

"I want only to find their location, then follow them with my trackers," the general continued. "But I won't come up on them and attack until I have been reinforced in the next few days. I'm afraid if your experience has taught me anything, it is that caution is the watchword."

Perry licked his lower lip. "I think we all have a newfound respect for their fighting abilities, sir."

"Besides discovering where the enemy is and where he is going, I also seek to honor those fallen men with a decent interment."

It made Perry's skin crawl to think of those bodies having lain in the open for the last nine days—bloating in the rising heat, blackening with decay. A fallen soldier deserved far better from his fellows.

AT SIX-THIRTY THAT Tuesday morning, barely an hour after sunrise, General Howard led his column of infantry, cavalry, and artillery out of that one-night bivouac at Johnson's ranch and started for the White Bird battlefield.

At the top of the hill, Howard had Arthur Chapman called over to the head of the march.

"Mr. Chapman, I'm putting you in charge of the Walla Walla volunteers."

"You got something in mind for us?" the dark-eyed civilian asked.

"A scouting mission," the general said. "To determine where the Nez Perce have gone."

"Very good, General," Chapman replied. He pointed off to the right of their line of march. "We'll push west till we reach the edge of the canyon, staying with the top of this ridge, where Colonel Perry and the rest of his men straggled out of the canyon the morning of the fight."

Perry asked, "Will that give you a good vantage point to look into the valley of the Salmon?"

But Chapman never looked at the captain. He merely nodded to Howard and answered, "None better. We'll have us a good look around for them red murderers for you, General."

Howard rocked back in the saddle, arching his back as if attempting to relieve a knotted muscle. "Very good. We'll be in the valley."

"Gonna bury them soldiers?" Chapman asked with a great deal of curiosity in his eyes.

"We're going to do what any God-fearing soldier would do for his fallen comrades."

Perry watched Chapman turn away without another word; then Howard spoke.

"Colonel, we'll leave Whipple's L Company and Captain Throckmorton's artillery unit in an advantageous spot at the top of White Bird Hill, perhaps over there."

"They'll cover our advance in the event of a surprise, sir?"

The general nodded. "Exactly." Then he turned to a knot of nearby officers. "Colonel Miller?"

The Massachusetts-born captain serving with the Fourth U. S. Artillery, Marcus P. Miller, urged his horse close to Howard's. "Sir?"

"You're assigned the advance as we enter the valley."

The captain saluted. "Yes, General. Captain Winters?"

Henry E. Winters wheeled his mount and approached. "Am I given the honor of supporting the colonel?" He used Miller's brevet rank.

"You are," Howard replied. "Colonel Perry and I will follow you down with the rest of the command. When we reach the battlefield, the colonel himself will organize the search for the bodies of his dead."

The first corpse they found startled the men in the advance with Miller and Winters. From a distance, the figure appeared to be an Indian hiding behind a bush, perhaps even pointing a weapon at the oncoming soldiers. While the rest of the column watched, Winters sent three men forward— their carbines held at ready, prepared to fire, all aimed at the rigid corpse. Up close they discovered that it wasn't an Indian at all, but a white man, his body standing, somehow attached to the spiny branches of a hawthorn bush—both arms outstretched as if he were clutching it.

"It's Sergeant Gunn," Perry grimly explained to Howard after they stopped near the remains of the gray-haired veteran. "F Company, sir."

"He sold his life dearly that day, Colonel."

Perry nodded, noticing the many copper cases in the grass near Gunn's feet. "Colonel Miller, assign three men to bury Sergeant Gunn."

The rest pushed on toward that distant ridge where Perry had deployed his battalion for their abbreviated battle against the screaming horsemen. After crossing another hundred yards, the captain realized he would never forget the grisly sight that greeted them this sunny Tuesday morning. While he was certain the terror of their frantic retreat would forever trouble his waking hours, Perry was just as certain the horror of what lay before him at this very moment would forever haunt his nights.

That and the unearthly stench.

Arms and legs frozen akimbo in death, twenty-some bodies lay scattered across the hillsides, every last one blackened by nine days of mortifying decay and a relentless summer sun, flesh grotesquely swollen with the gases of decomposition until most of the faces were totally unrecognizable in their horrid death grins.

Oh, the stench. When that morning's warm breeze suddenly died and the heavy air lay still upon that field of death, the pungent odor rose up to assault a man with a gagging ferocity.

Perry quickly dragged out his big bandanna and clamped it over his mouth and nose, remembering to breathe through his mouth. The next time the capricious breeze died, he felt his eyes beginning to water with the putrid stench of decaying flesh. His skin began to crawl as he pulled back on the reins and signaled a halt to Miller's and Winter's companies.

On both sides of Perry now the troopers came to a halt. He heard the quiet sounds as the men noisily swallowed, struggling to control their stomachs, while some audibly gagged. One man spilled off the side of his horse, collapsing to his knees as he retched himself free of his hearty breakfast of hardtack, sidemeat, and coffee. Most of it still undigested as it seeped into the grassy soil.

"Get that man back where the air is better," Perry ordered, his eyes streaming now with the very tangible sting of long-forgotten death, doing all that he could to keep from joining those who were gagging at the sight, at the stench, at the very sound of the big, bloated horseflies at work on the bloodied corpses.

Throbbing masses of insects blackened every dead soldier's eyes, waded their way around in his every wound, crawling in and out of the gaping nostrils, a'swim in every swollen, distorted mouth.

It almost appeared these dead were crying out, calling forth from the far side of eternity. . . .

He turned slightly, swallowed hard, and gave his orders. "C-Colonel Miller. Captain Winters. Bring up the infantry companies. Divide them and your men into three platoons each. One platoon from each company will be on burial detail at a time. The other two platoons from each company will remain in reserve, back where the breathing is a little better. Trowel bayonets. Is your mission understood?"

But Perry didn't really look at either of the officers for a response before he quietly, and quickly, concluded, "Do all that you can to give each man a decent burial, gentlemen."

Miller almost lost control as he nodded in answer. His tearing eyes held unabashed gratitude as he quickly turned aside and rode off to pass on the order to the infantry commanders.

Winters saluted, and swallowed hard. This Ohio-born officer had risen up through the ranks after enlisting in the First Cavalry in 1864. "Very good, Colonel. That way we can sp-spell the men."

One by one, the dismounted cavalrymen and foot soldiers located the bodies scattered in the tall, waving grass. It wasn't hard to find the dead.

Two or three soldiers sank to their knees beside a body and began scraping at the black soil with their trowel bayonets they pulled from the leather scabbards hanging from their 1876 pattern duty belts, which were fitted with fifty canvas cartridge loops. The three-man squads frequently spelled one another, as even the hardy were quickly forced to crawl away, retching, struggling to get upwind, to put some distance between them and the distorted remains until they could once again scratch at the ground, removing one small trowelful of soil at a time from what would be each fallen soldier's final resting place.

One small handful of dirt at a time. Scrape the ground with the trowel. Keep from heaving. Scoop the dirt out of the tiny hole. Gag a little. Scrape some more. Pull at the long roots of the tall, nutritious grasses. Scratch the loam from the shallow trench. Stop of a sudden and lunge away, gulping for air. Ashamed when your stomach won't obey and you gag on the burning contents of your breakfast as it hurtled on past your tonsils and over the back of your tongue.

Then you wiped your mouth on your sleeve and scraped some more, eyes burning, tearing spilling down your cheeks until you were almost blinded by the sting of the stench and could barely see.

How thankful Captain David Perry was that many of those men closest to the putrefying bodies had tears in their eyes, streams of them glistening down their cheeks. Right here no one would know exactly why he was crying among all these with tears in their eyes.

Merely looking at those bodies from F and H Companies. Men he might have recognized on the parade at Fort Lapwai had they lived through that fight on the White Bird. Nameless men who had died an ignoble death as the Nez Perce rolled up the left side of their line and hacked Perry's battalion to ribbons. Nameless, and now faceless, anonymous soldiers who had died here for their country . . . fighting an enemy that had surprised them all, rising up to show they were willing to die for their country.

One by one. By one. The hours crawled by with agonizing slowness because the burial details were often finding the swollen, mortifying bodies were unmanageable. As soon as the soldiers attempted to pull a corpse into a shallow grave, a leg or an arm tore free of the body already sticky, pasted to the grassy slope.

Because most of the dead had been stripped of outer clothing—boots, britches, and campaign blouse—every skull and every inch of bare flesh lying against the ground had begun to decay, so much so that when the burial parties dragged the corpses toward their final resting places, that flesh tore free. As hair was pulled free in the tangled, blood-crusted grass, it made many of the bodies appear as if they had been scalped or horribly mutilated by the victorious warriors.

Just the sight of those dismembered corpses, the blackened flesh ripped off and left clinging to the grass, was enough to cause men to begin retching anew.

From one group to another, Perry slowly rode among the burial parties, suggesting how the sergeants should proceed with their details.

"Dig the grave as close as you can to the body," he quietly told the noncoms from behind his bandanna. "Then do your best to roll the body into the hole."

"That way I won't pull off 'nother arm the way I just did," grumbled Sergeant Bernard Simpson, just before the First U. S. cavalryman had to swallow down a mouthful of bile. "S-sir."

"Do the best you can, Sergeant," Perry sympathized, feeling a touch of remorse for these men facing a horrid and daunting task. "Every man here understands we're all just doing for others what we'd want done for us."

CHAPTER SIX

———— ❄ ————

JUNE 26, 1877

THERE'S YOUR GODDAMNED MURDERIN' INJUNS FOR YOU!" BELLOWED Ad Chapman at the handful of "Captain" Tom Page's Walla Walla volunteers who had joined him in that ride due west along the high, bare ridge to reach this overlook where they could peer down into the valley of the Salmon.

"Those bastards are running south across the river!" exclaimed E. J. Bunker as they all squinted in the fading light as clouds rolled in to begin blotting out the sun.

Those half-naked horsemen the thirty-six-year-old Chapman had spotted across the Salmon could be no more than a small part of the village they had bumped into back on that bloody Sunday.

George Shearer rubbed an aching shoulder and growled, "I'll wager the squaws and nits've all crossed the river, fixin' to disappear in the mountains."

Chapman looked at his friend a moment, nodding. "Army never catch 'em once they get in that broke-up country other side of the Salmon."

"S'pose we oughtta get back to tell the general?" Bunker asked, his horse done blowing, starting to crop the short grasses on this nearly barren ridge top.

Chapman fished a plug of tobacco from his coat pocket. "If Howard's gonna have a ghost of a chance to get his hands on them Nez Perce, he'll have to quit his dawdling."

Bunker snorted, "That one-armed general still says he's gonna wait for more reinforcements before he'll attack that village again."

Chapman looked at each of their faces a moment, then said, "The way those red bastards fought us a few days back, might not be so bad an idea Howard has more men afore he jumps that camp. Let's get on down below— give that general the news he's been waiting to hear."

He rode tall in the saddle. Thin as a split rail and every bit as lean as a buggy whip. Chapman still had a full head of hair: black as the bottom of a tar spring did it spill across his shoulders. Born back east in Iowa, Chapman had been no more than seven years old when his family traipsed out to Oregon during that historic western migration along the Emigrant Road. His father would become one of the founders of Portland.

In this country rife with opportunity, nine-year-old Arthur had carried dispatches for the army between the Dalles and Fort Walla Walla during the

Rogue River Indian War. Six years later, young Chapman had settled over east in Nez Perce country, sending down roots in a piece of ground beside White Bird Creek, at the mouth of a stream that would one day soon bear his name. There he began raising cattle and breeding horses, as well as operating his ferry across the Salmon River at the mouth of the White Bird.

Then almost three years back he had sold his ranch to John J. Manuel and moved north to a new homestead he built on Cottonwood Creek some eight miles from Mount Idaho, out on the Camas Prairie, where he continued to breed horses. Over the last two weeks of Indian troubles, Chapman had lost some four hundred head of prime stock to Nez Perce raiding parties.

He'd had himself a checkered history with the tribe, sometimes friendly, ofttimes not. On the balance, he'd admit, mostly not so friendly. With that short fuse he had to his temper, Chapman hadn't been all that good a neighbor to the Nez Perce, even though he had married an Umatilla squaw a few years back. Even though he spoke real good Nez Perce, too. A few years back the couple had a young boy, and now his wife was expecting another child come early fall.

Problem was, hard as he tried, for the longest time Ad couldn't seem to win with either side—not with most of the Nez Perce, who distrusted him to one degree or another and not with most of the whites, who considered him a traitor because he had married an Indian woman and fathered a half-breed child.

Simple truth was, Chapman didn't endear himself to some folks simply because he called things as he saw them. To some white folks, that was downright heresy. A white man was supposed to stick up for a white man, no matter what.

But then, on top of that uneasiness, there was a story going the rounds that the Non-Treaty bands didn't trust him any farther than they could throw him because they claimed Chapman had stolen some of their cows and sold them off to Chinese miners up at Florence and Elk City in the mountains. Hell, if those Indians didn't take better care of their stock than to leave their cattle run through Chapman's upper pasture, they deserved to be missing a few cows!

Such was the delicate line he walked between the white world and red in this Salmon River country. For good or bad, there honestly wasn't a man who possessed more experience dealing with the Non-Treaty bands than Arthur Chapman. In fact, over the years, he had forged quite a bond with Chief Looking Glass and a few of his headmen. Ad figured when you got right down to it, his steadfast friendship with the old chief had to go a long way to showing the Nez Perce he wasn't so bad a white fella after all.

Why, on the Thursday before the White Bird massacre, two of his Nez Perce friends—Looking Glass and Yellow Bear—even rode over from the big traditional gathering the Non-Treaty bands were having at the head of Rocky Canyon on Camas Prairie to let Chapman know that some of the young bucks had gone on the warpath and had already killed seven white men by that time. Looking Glass said he was taking his people and moving back to their homes on the Clearwater, wanting to get away from the troublemakers. A damn honorable act by those two old Nez Perce friends to come warn him at a time like that, even going so far as to suggest that he clear out till things simmered down a bit. No sooner had he gotten his wife and son started away than the three of them spotted a war party headed for his ranch.

Chapman figured then and there he might well owe Looking Glass his life for that timely warning, since it turned out to be a horse race all the way to the outskirts of Mount Idaho. Sprinting into the tiny settlement barely ahead of those warriors screaming for his blood, Ad dropped out of the saddle in front of Loyal P. Brown's hotel and began spreading the alarm, shocking one and all with the first report of the Salmon River murders. By nightfall the folks flooding into town had formed their own militia company and elected Chapman as its captain.

In the predawn darkness of the following morning, June 15, Chapman had slipped out of town and back to his ranch to keep a planned rendezvous with Looking Glass and Yellow Bear. As the sky was graying just before five o'clock, he rode up to his friends, a bit surprised to find them accompanied by two other warriors. The chief grimly related the names of the settlers who had been killed up to that point in time on the Camas Prairie and along the Salmon, too. Good Indians they were, those Looking Glass people.

Ad was mightily relieved none of the Asotin band were involved with the murders or later on in the fight that left so many soldiers dead in the White Bird Canyon. Now if Looking Glass's people could manage to stay out of the way of Howard's army, the soldiers would quickly get the rest of those Non-Treaties mopped up and driven onto the reservation.

By the time Ad's civilians had backtracked along the high ridge, then picked their way down the west slope into the valley to reach the site of the army's White Bird debacle, the clouds were noticeably lowering. Distant thunder suddenly reverberated off the surrounding hills. Its long-dying rattle bouncing off the nearby slopes compelled many of the edgy soldiers to duck and scramble for their rifles, preparing for an attack by the Nez Perce.

An occasional finger of lightning starkly split the darkness with a brilliant display. As the civilians approached the first of the burial details, Ad noticed how the soldiers had tied bandannas over their faces, covering everything below their eyes as they tugged and rolled a bloated, distorted figure onto a gray army blanket, then dragged the corpse to the shallow trench they had scraped out of the rocky soil nearby. Hoisting up the four corners of the blanket, the four soldiers rolled the stinking remains into the hole.

One of the soldiers turned suddenly and fell to his knees, ripping off his bandanna as he violently puked into the grass.

Another soldier knelt over the sickened man, patting him on the back as the civilians rode up. He said to Chapman, "The critters been at this one."

"Critters?"

"Wolves, coyotes maybe?"

Chapman crossed his wrists over the saddlehorn and hunched forward. "Likely not wolves. Used to live right down yonder, mouth of that little creek. Maybeso it was a coyote got to that dead soldier—I've seen a mess of coyotes around here in my time. Still, I'd wager it was small critters ate on 'im. Racoons, maybe a badger. Chewed the poor fella up, did they?"

The soldier nodded as the first of the big drops started to fall out of the lowering sky. Then he gestured across the slope. "Some of the rest been et on, too."

Giving the blackening heavens a sidelong glance, Chapman said, "Rain comin'—I figger your work for the day is 'bout over now."

Gasping, the soldier on his knees replied, "Thank Jesus in Heaven for small b-blessings."

The tall soldier patted the man on the shoulder, then looked again at Chapman as a roll of thunder faded on down the canyon. "Sounds just like God in Heaven is firing a burial volley to honor our dead."

Sensing the hair rise on his arm with more than the dramatic electrical charge in the clean, damp air, Chapman gently nudged his horse away from the three soldiers.

He didn't know if he believed in God anymore. Not when such terrible things were happening to women and children, even to some men—folks who had never given hurt to any person. Couldn't be a God to his way of thinking.

Finding Howard taking cover temporarily beneath some streamside trees about the time the general was giving orders to suspend the burial duties with only eighteen of the dead interred, telling his officers that he intended for his command to return to Johnson's ranch for the night, Chapman and the volunteers reined up nearby and dragged out their rubber ponchos as the underbelly of the low sky opened up on them. While the rain grew serious, the small band of civilians dismounted to report sighting the warriors upriver, across the Salmon.

"They've crossed already," Howard grumped.

"You can't spend much time here, General," Chapman advised.

That made Howard's face go stony, cold. "These men deserve a decent burial, Mr. Chapman."

"Meantime, your prey gonna waltz on outta sight."

"I'll just have to take that chance, won't I?" Howard replied testily. Then he turned and pointed on down the narrow valley. "Whose place was that?"

"Used to be mine, General," Chapman began. "Sold it to John Manuel."

"Was he one of the victims of the Nez Perce depredations?"

"Him, and his wife, their youngest, a baby—all gone. No hide, no hair. Had a daughter, Maggie, too—"

"No, I saw her yesterday in Mount Idaho," Howard stated sadly. "Claimed Joseph killed her mother and baby brother."

Chapman regarded the heap of ruins, all that was left of the nearby buildings he had hammered together of a time years ago. "You wanna ride along, we go take a look for ourselves, General?"

Howard and a handful of officers readily agreed as the storm softened into a steady, soaking drizzle. For some time they inspected the blackened timbers that had caved in, digging around near the charred river stones of the chimney and fireplace that remained standing despite the destruction of the rest of the cabin.

"I found some bones, General," Chapman suddenly reported.

"The victims?"

"Naw." Ad shook his head as three of the civilians stepped over to expose more of the charred bones with the round toes of their tall boots. "Don't think so. These here bones ain't big enough to be human."

Howard sighed, arching his back in a stretch. "Look there. The Nez Perce raiders destroyed everything else . . . but that outhouse."

Chapman turned, chuckling to see his old single-seat outhouse still standing, sheltered back in the nearby timber. "Damn if that ain't the strangest thing. I'd figgered they'd at least tip it over on their way out, since they burned everything else to the ground."

"Maybeso them dumb Injuns don't know what a outhouse is for!" Bunker snorted.

"Let's go have us a look," Ad suggested.

Shearer and Bunker were already at the outhouse by the time Chapman and the officers had picked their way clear of the burned-out ruins of the Manuel house.

"Chapman!"

He jerked up to see Shearer frantically waving his good arm at the outhouse door they had flung open before them. As he watched, George and Bunker both bent to their knees in the open doorway, struggling with something.

"An Indian?" Howard asked.

"Ain't likely, General," Chapman replied as they both started trotting toward the nearby trees where the old structure stood all but surrounded by brush.

"Then that must surely be one of your men, a survivor, Colonel Perry," Howard said as the two civilians turned slowly, a third man suspended between them.

"My gawd!" Chapman said as he jerked to a halt before the trio, reaching out to raise the barely conscious man's chin. "It's John Manuel!"

"But his daughter said she saw him killed," David Perry declared. "Shot from his horse. She was wounded in the same attack."

"John. John," Chapman cooed, rubbing the man's skeletal cheeks with both of his damp hands.

The eyes fluttered, half-opening to stare at Chapman an instant before they snapped wide as twenty-dollar gold pieces.

"Ch-ch-ch—"

"Don't try to talk," Chapman reminded, still stroking the man's face.

"J-j-jen—"

"We don't know, John," Shearer admitted. "Ain't found Jennet's body."

"So she might still be alive," Ad said. "Maybeso your boy, too. Maggie's alive."

"M-Maggie?"

"She's waiting for you in Mount Idaho."

About that time Chapman noticed the wounds in Manuel's hips as the man's feet scuffed along the rain-soaked ground. Howard sent one of his aids to fetch a surgeon as the half-dead man's friends carried him toward a dry copse of trees where Shearer and Bunker eased Manuel to the ground. Over time that afternoon, with some hot coffee and a little salt pork fed him in small slivers, John J. Manuel told the story of his thirteen-day ordeal.

"Thirteen days?" Howard asked.

"This was one of the first places the bastards hit," Chapman growled.

With an arrow in the back of his neck, a bullet hole through both hips, Manuel had been hurtled off his horse into the brush where he lay still, feigning death as his wife and daughter attempted escape on foot. While he heard their screams and the war cries of the attackers, Manuel confessed there was nothing he could do. Unable to use his legs, he could only drag himself farther into the brush by pulling himself along with his arms.

By sundown on the second day he had managed to inch himself to the outhouse and crawl inside, where he listened to the comings and goings of horsemen for days on end. The sun rose, and the sun set. Over and over again. In the meantime, Manuel had managed to use his folding knife to dig at the four-inch iron arrow point embedded in the muscles of his neck, eventually working the barb free. It still lay on the plank floor of the outhouse, along with the blood-crusted knife Manuel had used in the surgery.

In the predawn darkness of the following morning, he had crawled from the tiny structure, back into the brush where he gathered horseradish leaves he stuffed inside his shirt before dragging himself back to the outhouse. There, Manuel explained, he had chewed the pungent, bitter leaves, crushing them into a poultice he then applied to his angry, infected wound. His frontier medicine had worked. Over the past eleven days the herbal poultice had eased the infection, and Howard's surgeon from Fort Walla Walla, George M. Sternberg, discovered that the once-ugly wound had begun to knit up nicely, without need for any sutures.

At night Manuel had ventured out, dragging himself through the darkness to the creek bank, where he slowly gathered wild berries, one at a time, and sipped at water he dipped from the White Bird in his cupped hand. With so little to sustain him through his ordeal, Manuel had progressively grown thinner and weaker, unable to venture from the outhouse these past five days.

Dr. Sternberg explained to the soldiers and civilians, "Chances are he would have died tomorrow, perhaps the next day, if we hadn't found him when we did."

"This is truly good news!" Howard exclaimed.

Chapman regarded the dimming light. "Too late now to start John back to the Johnson place. We'll take him on in to Mount Idaho come morning."

"He still won't be in any condition to ride," Sternberg declared.

"We'll make us a travois to pull him out of here," Chapman said as he stood. "George, you stay put with John. We'll do what we can to keep him dry for the night right here."

Howard cleared his throat authoritatively. "For the time being, Mr. Chapman, once you've seen to Mr. Manuel here, I suggest you use the rest of what light is left in the day to take your volunteers and search down to the mouth of the White Bird. See if you sight any more than those warriors you spotted from the ridge above."

As the drizzling rain sluiced from his wide-brimmed felt hat, Chapman nodded before he turned on his heel. Without a word he moved to his horse and rose to the saddle, setting off in the mist alone.

Even the sky was crying—either out of exultation at his finding an old friend still breathing . . . or out of some unimaginable grief for all those victims Chapman knew they never would find alive.

CHAPTER SEVEN

———✦———

JUNE 27–29, 1877

BY TELEGRAPH

———

More Details of the Great
Storm.

———

Causes of Idaho's Indian War.

———

Facts Regarding the Late Indian Outbreak.
SAN FRANCISCO, June 26.—A press dispatch from
Boise City says that Rev. T. Mesplie, for thirty
years a Catholic missionary among the Indian tribes of
Oregon, Washington, and Idaho, and now stationed at Fort
Boise as chaplain of the United States army, gives the
following intelligence in regard to Indian matters:
. . . In speaking of General Howard, Howlish Wampoo
said the Indian laughed at the general and his fine
speeches, saying he would never persuade them to give
up Wallowa valley, which they were resolved to keep at
every hazard. Father Mesplie says the chiefs and
principal men who inaugurated this war are rich and
influential, and that they will be able to draw to
their support all the disaffected Indians belonging
to the various tribes, and that these constitute a
majority in every case. He is of the opinion that
the war will be general and prolonged, as the Indians
have been long deliberating and preparing for it, and
have staked everything upon its issue. The father
says the Nez Perces number in all about four thousand.
Of this number about a hundred and fifty will remain
friendly or inactive. He estimates the number of
warriors which the Nez Perces can bring into the
field at 1,000 . . . Besides these there are
Flatheads and their confederates in Montana,
with whom the Nez Perces are in close alliance
. . . He obtains his data from accurate knowledge

acquired by long residence among the Indians. He
regards the liberty allowed the Indians to remain
off the reservations and the unrestricted
intercourse allowed between them and the whites
as the principal causes of the present outbreak.

Fort Lapwai
June 27, 1877

Dear Mamma,

*. . . Our little post is quiet today, but more troops will be here on
Saturday. Major Boyle, Mr. Bomus, and Doctor, along with
twenty men, are our entire garrison just now. All the rest are in
the front. General Howard sent in dispatches last night hurrying
up the troops. He wants to make an attack, and we all feel today
that there may be a fierce fight raging and many poor fellows
suffering not fifty miles from us. The Indians are in a horseshoe of
the Salmon River, a place with the most natural fortifications,
equal to the lava beds* of the Modocs, and we know them to be
well provisioned. They have at least five hundred head of cattle in
there, and quantities of camus root, which they use a great deal.
We hear this place has only one trail leading into it. So you see the
advantages they have. Oh, how I hope our commanders will be
cautious and not risk anything. I suppose General Howard has
out there now about four hundred men and some artillery, which I
don't suppose he will be able to use at all. Those four hundred men
are nearly the entire body of troops from this Department. The
army is so small at best, and the various companies are so small,
that it takes five or six companies to make a hundred men. None
of the companies, not even the cavalry, is full.*

*How glad I should be if I could pick up John and the babies
and get out of this region. I feel that nothing else will let me feel
calm and settled. My brain seems in a whirl, constantly seeing
the distress of these poor women who have lost their husbands,
and constantly expecting and fearing to hear from our friends
in the front, and also sort of half afraid for ourselves here. I
wonder if poor little Lapwai will ever seem peaceful and calm to
me again.*

*Do write soon . . . We all join in love, and I am glad you
are safe.*

Your loving daughter,
Emily F.

**Devil's Backbone*, vol. 5, the *Plainsmen* series.

MERCIFULLY, OVERNIGHT THE SOAKING RAIN HAD CLEANSED MUCH OF the stench from the air in that valley of death by the time Howard's troops returned early the next morning.

Second Lieutenant Sevier McClellan Rains had never been so happy to ride out of any place the way he had been happy to ride out of White Bird Canyon as the sun began to set yesterday. After a second night's bivouac at Johnson's ranch, the commanding general had everything packed up and ready to depart by 7:00 A.M. on the morning of the twenty-seventh. It continued to rain past dawn, a slow, steady weeping from a low gray sky. The young lieutenant dreaded ever returning to this valley of such unspeakable death.

As they had on Tuesday, the various cavalry and infantry companies again worked over the battlefield in platoons, searching the ravines and the thickets for the remains of fallen soldiers. While the rain kept down the revolting stench, the unrelenting showers soon soaked every man through to the skin, making them all as miserable as could be. So it was with no little eagerness that Rains looked forward to taking his nine men for a ride back up a sidewall of the canyon to search a narrow ravine for any of Perry's soldiers who might have fallen during their mad retreat back up White Bird Hill.

Born in Michigan, this young officer had graduated from West Point only the year before, a mere ten days before the Custer massacre in June of '76. Prior to graduation, Rains had applied for an appointment to the Fourth Cavalry, a move endorsed by the regimental commander, Colonel Ranald S. Mackenzie. Instead, Rains was assigned to the First Cavalry, disappointed that he would have to serve in the Northwest instead of on the Great Plains fighting the Sioux and Cheyenne. A cavalry officer by schooling, who now found himself thrust into a dirty little Indian war out here in Nez Perce country, vigorous and energetic, Rains was itching to show his superiors just what he was made of—

His horse snorted. Almost immediately his nose had found them. Even before any of the men spotted the bodies.

"How many of 'em are there?" one of the soldiers asked the other enlisted men arrayed behind Rains as they all scratched into their pockets for bandannas and handkerchiefs.

"I count eight, soldier," the lieutenant answered. "Eight of them."

The bloated corpses were strewn at the head of a short dead-end ravine. Six of them clustered together in a bunch. One of them lay by itself out by the mouth of the ravine. And the last man sat up alone against the end of the ravine, propped with his back to the grassy wall. The end of the line.

"Look there, sir!" exclaimed Private Franklin Moody, a member of Rains's own L Company, First U. S. Cavalry. "He's a lieutenant. Just like you."

"Hard to tell, but that's Theller, soldier," Rains replied quietly, looking down on his fellow officer, staring transfixed at the bullet hole between the eyes. "Lieutenant Edward R. Theller."

"I don't 'member him, sir. He First Cavalry, was he?" asked Private David Carroll as he inched up to stop at Rains's elbow.

"No, soldier. Theller was detached from the Twenty-first Infantry to go along with Colonel Perry's battalion when it marched away from Fort Lap-wai."

Nearby, Private Otto H. Richter whistled in amazement. *"Mein Herr—*lookit the cawtridges."

"Das right, Otto. Dese fellas dun't give up easy," said Private George H. Dinteman in his stilted English. "Did dey, sir?"

Rains shook his head, continuing to stare at Theller's face, then at those copper cases scattered around him and the others, but always, always return-ing to that bullet hole in the middle of the lieutenant's forehead where the flies had busily laid their eggs. Another day, two at the most, these bodies would be crawling with wormy maggots. Again, as always, he came back to staring at that single bullet hole.

"We bury dem hare, zir?" asked Private Frederick Meyer in troubled English dripping with a thick German accent.

The steady rain overnight had made the ground soft. Rains tore his eyes from that bullet hole for a moment while he screwed his boot heel into the soil. "Yes," the young lieutenant told them. "Maybe one common grave is the best idea. Let's do that—over there at the mouth of the ravine. Those two with their fatigue britches still on—check their pockets for personal effects that the surviving families might wish to receive from Colonel Perry. We'll work in squads of three, spell each other like yesterday."

He went on to have the three Germans start: Richter, Dinteman, and Meyer. Good, solid men. Not particularly fast with any mental wizardry, but good, dependable soldiers. Not given to any complaining about this nasty work with the decomposing, stinking bodies. Once the three had started work on the mass grave for all eight men and the rest either started digging through the pockets of those two who still had some clothing on their bodies or simply plopped down in the wet grass to wait their turn at the trowel bay-onets, the young lieutenant turned around once again to stare at the face of that other young lieutenant in this narrow ravine.

And that single bullet hole between the eyes.

Yes, indeed, soldiers, he thought in silence. *Look at all those cartridge cases around them. These eight men sold their lives dearly that bloody Sunday morning. Retreating from the battlefield, they must have ducked up this short, narrow ravine to take some cover from the bare naked hillside—only to discover they were trapped in a box.*

"Private Carroll!" he called out, turning to speak over his shoulder. "I want you and Moody to begin gathering some stones."

"Stones, Lieutenant?" Franklin Moody asked.

"Rocks. Anything small enough for you to pull out of the ground and carry over here."

David Carroll asked, "You gonna lay 'em on the grave, sir?"

"Yes. Maybe they will keep the predators from digging up the remains once we're gone," Rains explained. "Once they're left here . . . to lie alone for all eternity."

The two privates shuffled off murmuring between themselves.

How would it be, Rains wondered, to have been Theller in his final moments? To find himself trapped with his small squad of men, surrounded and outnumbered, with no way out but to make the Nez Perce warriors pay dearly . . . pay very, very dearly for each soldiers they would kill that day?

By the time the mist turned into a steady rain, falling harder, the men had begun to drag the first of the bodies into the long, shallow trench made big enough for eight bloated corpses. As all nine men in his burial detail began to quickly scoop the rich, damp soil back over the distorted remains, young Lieutenant Sevier M. Rains pulled off his soggy hat and stood above them on the side of that ravine—just over his nine muddy, soaked soldiers as they struggled with those eight dead, bloated victims—quietly murmuring his Presbyterian prayers, words he had learned by heart while still a boy in rural Michigan.

As the strong-backed Germans and the wiry Irishmen stood, one by one, stretching the kinks out of their muscles there beside the bare, muddy ground, having placed a layer of rocks over the common grave, Rains began the prayer he hoped they all would join him in reciting.

". . . Forgive us of our trespasses . . . as we forgive those who trespass against us . . ."

BY TELEGRAPH

———

MONTANA.

———

Reports in Regard to the Flat Head
Indians.
DEER LODGE, Montana, June 27.—To Governor Potts, Helena: I am in receipt of the following from Postmaster Dickinson, of Missoula, Montana: Monday, June 26.—Rev. John Summers and Mr. Wilkins, who have just arrived from Corvallis, report that a Nez Perces, who talks good English, came from Lewiston, and says the Indians are coming into Bitter Root, and will come into the head of the valley and clear it out, and if the Flat Heads don't join them they will clear them out too. The Flat Heads have driven all their horses out of the valley, and the squaws and children are going up Lolo fork. A Nez Perces chief told Major Whaley that the Nez Perces were going to clear out the Bitter Root valley, and that the Flat Heads would join them on the 1st, as near as I can remember . . .

Fort Lapwai
June 29, 1877

My Dear Mamma,

I would give the world and all to see you, but I guess we will have to wait until the Doctor takes us in. I hope and pray the time will pass quickly until our time here is over, and that we will all be spared to meet again.

This horrible Indian war hangs over me like a gun. I can't shake it off and am daily expecting the Doctor will be ordered to join the troops in the field. We are all very anxious here. The dispatches that came in last night told us the troops were in sight of the Indian stronghold. I shall hope and pray that I shan't have to come home to you, after all, without my dear husband. Poor Mrs. Theller is still waiting here. She won't leave until she can get her husband's body. This losing one's husband in this way seems too horrible to think about. I can't help feeling how awfully hard it would be to lose my dear John any way, but that way would be hardest of all.

Your loving daughter,
Emily F.

CHAPTER EIGHT

JUNE 27–JULY 1, 1877

BY TELEGRAPH

Daring Postoffice Robbery at
Manhattan, Kansas.

IDAHO.

The Indian Situation—Telegram from
Gen. Howard.
SAN FRANCISCO, June 29.—A Portland press
dispatch says Colonel Wood has just received the
following dispatch from General Howard, dated at
the front, June 27, 8:45 A.M.: We have overtaken
Joseph, who is well posted at the mouth of White
Bird creek. Chief White Bird has been in charge of
the entire united bands of Joseph and is the fighting
chief. The Indians are bold and waiting for us to
engage them. Lieutenant Trumbull and volunteers
are at Slate creek. Our headquarters to-night will
be at the mouth of White Bird creek. The rains are
very troublesome; roads and trails bad; troops in
best of spirits and ready for decisive work.

FTER SPENDING THEIR SECOND DAY ON THE WHITE BIRD BATTLEFIELD, General Oliver O. Howard ordered his column on down White Bird Creek to its mouth, where they turned left and marched south, up the Salmon River, approximately two miles before finding enough open ground to bivouac the command. Late that afternoon as the first pickets were being established on his perimeter, A, D, G, and M batteries of the Fourth Artillery and C Company of the Twenty-first Infantry rumbled in to join the command.

"In memory of the slain officer, this will be recorded as Camp Theller," Otis told his united officer corps that evening after supper as the rain continued to pour down upon his column. "It's from here that we will begin our chase of the fleeing hostiles."

While the constant rain continued to batter the oiled canvas awning lashed over their heads, Howard went on to explain that, come morning, he was dispatching Captain David Perry back to Fort Lapwai for more ammunition and rations.

"This has more and more the appearance of a long campaign," he said regretfully, "longer than I would have anticipated on the day we departed Lapwai. But, with the additional reinforcements, we now have more than five hundred and thirty men, which include some sixty-five volunteers. In fact, 'Captain' William Hunter and his band of volunteers just arrived from Dayton, in Washington Territory. Accompanying them down from Lapwai, I'm most pleased to welcome Lieutenant Wood to my staff. Lieutenant, please take a step forward so all the men can get a look at you."

The slight, good-looking Wood eased into the center of that half-circle of cavalry and infantry officers. Nodding several times to the others, he then stepped over to stand near the commanding general.

"Mr. Wood will serve as my aide-de-camp for the remainder of the campaign."

SECOND LIEUTENANT CHARLES Erskine Scott Wood found it very difficult to sleep that night. Not that it was too cold or too damp for his tastes. Just that he constantly reminded himself to sleep light for fear of a surprise attack from the Nez Perce rumored to be right across the river from Camp Theller.

He finally gave up and crawled out of his bedroll after midnight. From the sounds of his snoring, General Howard was sleeping soundly in his tent nearby, so Wood lit a small candle and unbuckled the straps on his haversack. Reaching inside, he pulled out the spanking new leather-bound ledger book he had recently purchased in Lewiston on his way to the front. Positioning it across his thighs, Charles pulled a long pencil from the breast pocket he had had sewn inside his field blouse, then made the first entry on that very first page of his field diary.

> Overtook the main column, gentlemanly officers looking like herders, rough aspect of everyone, business not holiday costumes—
>
> Camp—singing, story telling and swearing, profanity—carelessness, accepting things—horrible at other times—as a matter of course. . . . Again there is the necessary leaving of last messages for sweet hearts, mothers, and wives, telling of jokes about being killed, about not looking for "my body" &c firing expected tomorrow. . . .
>
> Rain—eternal rain—veal & no veal—supper in camp. Visiting the different messes, youngsters with neither bedding nor shelter, rough it jokingly—night duty, posting the pickets—rough times all night standing in the rain—no fire—no talking, no bedding—no sleeping.

When next he tried to sleep, Wood had eventually drifted off, none-theless kept restless at first by the distant howl of coyotes in the nearby hills. Most of the officers and most of the soldiers had long ago learned that just such a howl had been heard by many of Perry's men as they sat in the dark, waiting out the coming of dawn and their disastrous attack. To most every man in Howard's command, those calls from the hills in the dark on that rainy night could come from only Nez Perce scouts keeping an eye on the camp . . . perhaps even signaling everything in readiness for their attack.

Finally able to sleep deeply, the young lieutenant was abruptly awak-ened by a gunshot just past midnight. That single report was followed by lots of loud noises from men angry and frightened at being caught off-guard in the middle of the night with what they thought was a wholesale attack by Nez Perce warriors.

As it turned out, in the melee and confusion, the camp was not under assault. Instead, a picket returning to his company had been mistaken for an enemy by a groggy, half-sleepy lieutenant jostled into that frightening reac-tion. The wounded soldier lingered in great pain until morning. Just past daybreak, he was buried nearby before the command prepared to move upriver.

Lieutenant Wood found another moment to scratch at his diary beside his breakfast fire.

> The alarm sounded at midnight—one of our own
> pickets shot by one of our men.* Up at 2 o'clock for
> fear of Indian habits of attack—roll call at 6.

That Thursday morning, the twenty-eighth of June, Howard moved his column up the Salmon to Horseshoe Bend, where his troops began prepara-tions to cross the river, following the trail of the fleeing Non-Treaty bands. Wood and others studied the swift, deep current and secretly wondered if the general would get his command across without incident utilizing the cable ferry Howard planned to employ after sending a pair of Nez Perce scouts across the river, dragging the ropes behind them.

But before they could even send the friendlies into the river, more than eighty-five warriors appeared on the hills across the Salmon, racing their horses down to the west bank, shouting, screaming, and firing their rifles. In another explosion of pandemonium, the soldiers dived this way and that for their weapons, precipitating another long-distance shooting match. Within minutes the noisy skirmish was over and the enemy horsemen were on their way, turning downriver to disappear beyond a nearby slope, with no appar-ent casualties on either side.

"The general has decided it was only a ruse, a diversion," Wood reported to the companies spread out along the east bank of the Salmon. "They only

---

*Most Indian Wars historians now agree that the lieutenant who was startled in his sleep and shot the returning picket was, in fact, Charles E. S. Wood himself.

want to keep us from crossing, to give their village more time to disappear into the heights on the other side. We must keep working as quickly as possible to get the command across!"

As hard as the men worked against the confines of those steep canyon walls, against the boiling current of the Salmon now in its full strength with spring runoff, it was not until the next morning, 29 June, when the column began its crossing.

But it would take them the whole of three long summer days to force their way across the mighty Salmon before they could even think about slogging into the wild and rugged hills on the other side.

HE WAS NOT your young, excitable sort. Not this Stephen Gerard Whipple. Forty years old, repeatedly described as "reliable" in reports written by his superiors, this captain had been the officer selected to march two companies of cavalry into the Wallowa valley earlier in the spring while Joseph and Ollokot were attending a peace parley with General O. O. Howard at Fort Lapwai. It was from his cantonment located at the western approaches to the Wallowa country that he had brought in his battalion, along with "Captain" Tom Page and his twenty-one volunteers from the town of Walla Walla.

Of moderate height and strongly built, Whipple had a presence about him, stemming mostly from his dark-browed, steely gaze. Born in upstate Vermont, the captain had been living on the West Coast when the Civil War erupted. He had served out the war with the California infantry, where he rose to the rank of lieutenant colonel, saw extensive duty on the frontier, and held a brevet for "faithful and meritorious service." About a year and a half after Appomattox, Whipple received a commission as captain in the Thirty-second Infantry, but in December of 1870 he requested, and was awarded, a transfer to the First U. S. Cavalry.

Whipple was again the man Howard would now choose for another lonely, dangerous, and ultimately fateful mission.

"I want you to take two companies of cavalry and arrest Looking Glass," the general stated not long after sunset the night before.

"A-arrest him, General?"

For a moment, Howard ground his teeth as if in exasperation at searching for an explanation, then declared, "For some weeks it has appeared that Looking Glass and his band of Alpowai were going to be peaceful. But now intelligence has been brought to me from our friendlies, reports showing that the chief and his headmen are leaning toward joining the hostiles."

Whipple wagged his head. "But . . . don't we have a reliable report that Looking Glass left the other bands after the murders began?"

"Yes," and Howard nodded, watching the light fade behind the tall mountains on the other side of the Salmon. "We were told he and his band wanted nothing of the war Joseph, White Bird, and the rest were starting."

"So—with all due respect, General—why am I to arrest Looking Glass now?"

The general's eyes narrowed; he was clearly not a man comfortable with having his decisions questioned. "Because some of the friendlies say he and his people are turning toward the hostiles. I've just received news that Looking Glass may have supplied at least twenty warriors to those who butchered Perry's command on the White Bird. There's a credible report that he's become a turncoat now, intending to join the hostiles himself at the first favorable opportunity."*

> More reports from four Mount Idaho citizens reached Howard that there was substantial evidence to show that warriors from Looking Glass's band had sacked two other homesteads: one belonging to Idaho County Commissioner George Dempster, and the other to James T. Silverwood. In addition, warriors had driven off stock. When the four whites attempted to approach the Looking Glass camp on Clear Creek, they were motioned to stay away in a hostile manner. In the minds of most white citizens, the Alpowai were clearly up to no good.
>
> Even Inspector Erwin C. Watkins of the Indian Bureau wrote Howard that Looking Glass was "running a recruiting station for Joseph."
>
> As history turns out, Howard's "friendlies" were actually two Mount Idaho civilians, Ezra Baird and Robert Nugent, who rode to Lewiston to excite the populace and local newspaperman with their tales that the Looking Glass people had declared war on the whites, intending to start hostilities in a few days!

Whipple gestured across the river at the west bank of the Salmon. "So we can't afford to have him and his warriors join up with the rest who are running loose over there in the Clearwater country."

It was evening on the twenty-ninth, the first day of those three it would take Howard to get his column across the turbulent current.

"Exactly, Captain. Looking Glass's people live and tend their gardens, graze their cattle, and breed their horses on their traditional grounds somewhere along the Clearwater."

"Yes, sir—I know the place."

"Technically, the Alpowai reside inside the reservation boundaries . . . but they've never signed any of the treaties."

---

*Howard and history do not clearly indicate how he reached these conclusions about Looking Glass's band, with the exception of the rampant rumors being circulated by Lewiston *Teller* editor Alonzo Leland, who repeatedly alleged in those days following the White Bird debacle: "Indian runners and Chinamen say the Looking Glass band has been increased in numbers, that they have plundered Jerome's place at the Clearwater bridge, that their whole movements indicate hostile intention though they pretend to yet be friends to the whites."

"Are some of the Christian bands nervous about the sympathies of the Looking Glass people, now that hostilities have broken out?"

"That's a mild way of putting it, Captain," Howard declared. "I've decided to arrest the chief and contain his people long enough to turn them over to the Mount Idaho volunteers."

"You really want to put them in the care of the citizens, General?" Whipple challenged. "Isn't that like turning over a canary to the care of the house cat?"

Howard appeared to bristle at this unvarnished questioning of moral sensibility of his planned arrest. "It will only be for a short time, Captain Whipple," he grumbled assuredly. "They will be in the care of the volunteers only until I can bring in the rest of these Non-Treaty troublemakers."

"You figure to catch up to them and drive them back across in this direction, General?"

"With you having the Looking Glass band under control on the east, and I herding Joseph from the west—we'll have them all onto the reservation within a week's time."

"As your order, sir. I'll draw four days' rations and sufficient ammunition for my march tonight, then depart in the morning."

"I would prefer that you leave before dawn, Captain."

Whipple nodded, sensing even more the importance of this mission. "We don't want to give Looking Glass or his henchmen any more time for making trouble."

"You might remember that I'm sending Colonel Perry back to Lapwai in the morning. He'll be covering part of the same trail up to Camas Prairie, where you'll turn off."

"To bring up more reinforcements from his post, General?"

"No," Howard answered. "He's taking the pack train with him to pick up more supplies and ammunition . . . on the outside chance that this campaign to drive the hostiles back across the Salmon takes longer than a week. In the final analysis, Looking Glass's band inhabits the country near my supply lines. So no matter what way you look at it, Captain—I must take care of him before I subdue the others."

Whipple's cavalry battalion moved out beneath a leaden sky before first light on the morning of 30 June, marching back down the Salmon to the mouth of the White Bird, then groping their way along the creek, moving east to the divide and over to Mount Idaho, where, during a short stop that afternoon that allowed the men time to eat and rest their horses, twenty civilians under "Captain" D. B. "Darius" Randall enthusiastically volunteered their services in helping to arrest Looking Glass. It was as plain as the brass on his buttons that these volunteers were itching to get a little revenge on the Nez Perce who had murdered so many friends of theirs. But Whipple was certain he could control them, and if the unthinkable happened . . . all the better to have more rifles along. One of the older volunteers, J. A. Miller, offered his services as an interpreter.

With the addition of these civilians, the captain felt nothing but confidence that he and his officers could handle what might be thrown their way. Accompanying Whipple's L Company was Captain Henry E. Winters in command of E Company. Serving with Winters were First Lieutenant Albert G. Forse—an 1865 graduate of the U. S. Military Academy, who had spent the last ten years serving with the First Cavalry in the Northwest— and Second Lieutenant William H. Winter, who graduated in 1872 and was promptly thrown into the Modoc War in southern Oregon.

In order to be on Looking Glass's doorstep at dawn on the first of July, Whipple ordered his detail men back into the saddle as the sun began to set that thirtieth day of June. Leaving behind their two .45-caliber Gatling guns and a detail of four men to operate those weapons in Mount Idaho so they could travel all the faster without the encumbrance of those prairie carriages, the eighty-seven men set off north, their objective some twenty-five miles away. Angling across the extreme southeastern corner of the Camas Prairie as the light faded, they struck the South Fork of the Clearwater, fully intending to make quick, efficient work of their warrant from Howard to prevent more of Looking Glass's warriors from joining up with those hostiles to whom Howard was preparing to give chase.

No matter the black of that moonless night, despite the ruggedness of the hills as they picked their way down one grade, then up a long, difficult slope to reach the high ground that rose abruptly along the east side of the Clearwater, Captain Steven Whipple pushed on, fully intending to catch the sleeping village unawares and completely unprepared at the peep of day.

CHAPTER NINE

Khoy-Tsahl, 1877

BY TELEGRAPH

The President Once More in
Washington.

Harvard Wins the Boat Race.

Latest From the Idaho
Indian War.

OREGON.

Latest from the Scene of Indian Hostilities.
SAN FRANCISCO, June 30.—A Portland press dispatch
gives the latest reports from the scene of the Indian
outbreak . . . It is reported that the Clear Water
Indians, under Looking-glass, had turned loose and
plundered George Dempster's place, between the middle
and south forks of the Clear Water, and driven off all
the stock of the settlers between these forks, and had
it at their camp about six miles above Kamiah. They
confirm Jim Sawyer's statement made in the Indian
council yesterday at Lapwai as to the purposes of
Looking-glass and his forty men. These Indians told
two Chinamen on Clear Water that they had declared war
against the whites, and would commence their raids upon
the inhabitants within ten days. When this news reached
Mount Idaho a force of twenty volunteers started
immediately for Clear Water, but no news
has come from them yet.
General Howard was notified and said that he would
send a detachment of regulars to scour the country in
that direction this morning. The volunteers who were
in the fight on White Bird saw the Indian who went out
as one of the friendly Indians with Col. Perry from
Lapwai beckon the hostiles forward to the fight, and

saw other movements of some friendly Indians evincing
their privity with the hostiles. During the fight a
report, which lacks confirmation, was received that
General Howard had attacked Joseph and dislodged
him from Horse Shoe Ridge . . .

B IRD ALIGHTING, CALLED *PEOPEO THOLEKT* BY HIS PEOPLE, SUCKED ON
the stringy beef Looking Glass's sister had boiled her brother for
an early breakfast that morning. In a matter of days the women
would have more of the camas roots and *kouse* dried so that they
could cook those roots in the boiling pots, along with the beef and what
game the men brought back to their people at this traditional camp they
called *Kamnaha** on the east bank of Clear Creek.** It wasn't a large camp,
this village of Looking Glass.

After about a dozen young hot-bloods rode away to join the war against
the wishes of their chief, the only men left numbered no more than four-
times-ten. The women and children counted up to three times that. They
were a small, yet prosperous, band.

Even though their traditional camping grounds lay within the boundaries
of the shrunken reservation the Shadows had marked off for his *Nee-Me-Poo*
people, these Alpowai had refused to sign what they called the Thieves'
Treaty of 1855 and agreed to the subsequent land steal of 1863. Unlike the
Christians who lived close to the whites up at Lapwai with Lawyer's many
friends, Looking Glass's people were traditional. They were Dreamers, not
Christians. Since this was the white man's special religious day, many of Looking Glass's Dreamers were away from camp, having gone downriver to Kamiah
to attend a traditional Dreamer service. Which meant that no more than half of
their men, only two-times-ten, remained in camp this quiet morning.

One big difference between those Lawyer Christians and the Looking
Glass Dreamers—the traditional people felt compelled by their ancestors to
hold onto what had never been theirs to give away, much less theirs to sell.

This was their land. And they meant no white man any harm as they
went about living their lives in the old way.

Eh-heh, there was no question that some of the younger men had slipped
away despite Looking Glass's scolding of those war-making chiefs at *Tepahlewam*, despite his repeated warnings not to foment trouble for the camp in
those first heady days after killing so many soldiers at *Lahmotta.*†

Bird Alighting, like Looking Glass and other leaders, knew that some of
their young men had raided one, perhaps two, of the Shadow homesteads in
the valley of the Clearwater. But the warriors claimed no Shadows were
harmed in their fun. Truth was, no white people were still around. They had
already fled south to Mount Idaho or Kamiah to the north or farther still—
running all the way to Fort Lapwai or Lewiston.

No white men hurt in that first frantic burst of young men raids. Only

---

*A Nez Perce term that cannot be translated.
**Approximately six miles above present-day Kooskia, Idaho.
†A Nez Perce term for White Bird Canyon.

houses and barns burned. Horses and cattle stolen, then driven back to this camp on Clear Creek. When matters had quieted down, Looking Glass and men like Bird Alighting vowed they would return what cattle and horses they could to their rightful, white owners. Until then, the *Nee-Me-Poo* would graze the animals and care for them. They had every reason to believe that by the middle of the summer moon all things would have returned to normal. Chances were good the Salmon River murderers would be caught and punished by the Shadows and Looking Glass's people would go back to living their lives in the same old way.

Which meant going to the *Moosmoos Illahe*—the buffalo country—every year or so to visit their friends the *E-sue-gha*.* Some of the *Nee-Me-Poo* referred to that tribe by the name of *Tsaplishtake*, or "Pasted On" people, because of their practice of making their hair longer by gluing on longer strands. Perhaps that meant they would help these friends fight the bellicose Lakota again, as they had in summers past, returning home to Idaho with their horses and travois sway-backed under the weight of buffalo hides scraped for lodge covers or tanned into hair-on robes for winter sleeping.

Looking Glass had become a hero in the faraway buffalo country. Once he had helped his old allies the *E-sue-gha* in a fight against the Lakota. That was a good country, Bird Alighting thought. That *E-sue-gha* land was good country. At the least a good second choice to this one. If the *Nee-Me-Poo* had to journey another place to find the buffalo, then that country beyond the high mountains was a good one—

"Soldiers are here!"

At that warning cry ringing outside the lodge, Bird Alighting spit out the long piece of meat he was chewing and bolted to his feet beside Looking Glass. They both shot out the doorway to stand among the many frightened people come to hear this news.

"Where?" someone shouted to those women on the creek bank who had given the warning and were pointing.

"Across!" a woman yelled, motioning to the far side of Clear Creek.

Bird Alighting saw them creeping down the steep hillside, sure enough. Perhaps ten times all his fingers. Not every one of them dressed in soldier clothes, so some of these Shadows—the white men who had no soul—were settlers, wagon men, or miners who scratched in the ground for the yellow rocks. Come to help the *suapies* or merely come to watch—either way . . . the arrival of all these white men bode no good for Looking Glass's peaceful camp. But *Peopeo Tholekt* tried to squeeze that fear out of his mind. After all, Looking Glass was known to those Mount Idaho Shadows—for just last year before he left for the buffalo country, the chief had delivered a speech in which he pledged friendship to the whites.

Seizing his friend by the shoulder, Looking Glass suddenly spun Bird Alighting aside. Leaning his face close, the chief instructed, "Go to these *suapies*. Find the soldier chief and say to him, 'Leave us alone. We are living here peacefully and want no trouble.' Tell him my hands are clean of white

---

*The Crow, or Absaroka, tribe of Montana.

man's blood and I want him to know they will remain clean. The other chiefs have acted like fools in murdering white men. Tell him I will have no part in such things and I will have nothing to do with such chiefs.' "

Bird Alighting nodded, saying, "I'll go fetch my horse, Looking Glass."

The chief wagged his head adamantly, squeezing Bird Alighting's arm. "No time! Take mine," and he bent to untie the long lead rope attached to his prize horse picketed to one of the lodge stakes.

"I will go tell them to leave us be."

Bird Alighting felt his stomach flutter and his heart pound mightily beneath his breastbone as he eased Looking Glass's horse across the creek and onto the grassy bank on the far side, continuing to the slope of the hill where the soldiers and Shadows waited. Which one was leader—

One of the soldiers immediately urged his horse forward. Three more of the *suapies* joined him, as well as two of the plain-dressed Shadows. Settlement or wagon men, for sure, Bird Alighting thought.

To his surprise, one of those wagon men spoke the *Nee-Me-Poo* tongue reasonably well. "Hello!" he called in a friendly tone that belied the misgivings *Peopeo Tholekt* felt to his marrow.

Bird Alighting turned to that left end of the small group where the two settlement men sat astride their horses. He began telling the Shadow what his chief wanted him to say: "Leave us alone. We are living here peacefully and want no trouble—"

He was interrupted as the second wagon man suddenly raised his rifle and shoved its muzzle right into Bird Alighting's ribs, pressed just below his left nipple so hard that it made the warrior wince.

At the same time, the Shadow angrily growled something Bird Alighting did not understand, but it nonetheless looked and sounded like a squint-eyed demand. Still, he did not know exactly what this man wanted. Maybe nothing more than to pull the trigger on his gun and blow a hole through Bird Alighting's heart—and he was afraid because he smelled the heavy stench of the white man's whiskey on the Shadow's every word.

Before Bird Alighting could protest or twist himself away from the gun's muzzle and the strong whiskey breath, that first settler—the *Nee-Me-Poo* talker—shoved the barrel downward, shouting at the bad-talker in some Shadow words Bird Alighting did not completely understand.

"This is not Looking Glass. Only a messenger, goddammit."

That's when the soldier chief asked something and the *Nee-Me-Poo* talker explained to Bird Alighting, "Go back to your camp and tell Looking Glass we want to talk to *him*. Talk only to him. Not a messenger like you. Talk to Looking Glass."

By the time Bird Alighting had turned Looking Glass's horse around and it was scrambling back up the east bank of Clear Creek, he could see how excited the men and women in the village had become. They had witnessed how the gun was shoved into his ribs. Maybe even heard the bad, loud talk from the Shadow. If they could not understand the words, then it wasn't at all difficult to understand the meaning—from both the tone and the strident volume of such angry talk.

As he reined the war pony among those eleven lodges, Bird Alighting saw that one of the older men was propping a new lodgepole against Looking Glass's lodge. But this pole had a big white cloth attached to it: well known as the Shadow signal for making peace, for talking truce—a signal for not making a fight.

"*Peopeo Tholekt!*" Looking Glass shouted, shuffling forward on foot. He held his bare hands aloft, imploring his friend, "Why aren't they leaving our country? Why are the *suapies* still here?"

"The soldier chief wants to speak only to you."

Looking Glass's face instantly went gray with worry. "This cannot be good. Go back now, and tell them my words again. Maybe they did not understand you good enough. Tell them once more that I want no trouble and to go away. We hurt no one, and want no one to bother us."

Back across the creek among the five Shadows, Bird Alighting was desperate for his words to take effect this time. "Looking Glass is my chief. I bring you *his* words. He does not want a war! He came back here to our country to get away from the other chiefs who would do wrong, come back here to escape war. He says: Do not cross to our side of the little river. We do not want any trouble with you! So go and leave us live in peace."

Grown even more red-faced than before, the angry civilian jabbed his rifle muzzle all the harder into Bird Alighting's ribs this second time. And once more that mean-eyed Shadow growled foul-sounding words the messenger could not understand. Again the friendly talker interceded, shoving the loud-talker's rifle aside, urging his horse forward, putting himself between the bad-talker and Bird Alighting for some modest protection. While Bird Alighting kept his eyes on the bad-talker, the good Shadow spoke in their foreign tongue to the soldier chief.

Finally, the Indian talker said in *Nee-Me-Poo*, "The rest of the soldiers will come with us when we come across the little river to speak—"

"No, Looking Glass says for the soldiers to stay on this side. Do not come across. Leave us alone—"

"The soldier chief wants to talk with Looking Glass," he interrupted sharply, as if losing patience. "If it makes it better, you tell him just the five of us will come across to talk. No more."

"All right," Bird Alighting replied with a little relief, turning the chief's horse around for the swollen creek.

He looked over his shoulder as the angry Shadow started to harangue all the others left behind on the bank. More loud voices joined his, primarily those of the other wagon and settlement men. None of the soldiers joined in the red-faced yelling. The next time Bird Alighting glanced over his shoulder, the angry one was shaking his rifle at the soldier chief and Shadows in the creek—but especially he shook it menacingly at Bird Alighting.

It took only minutes for them to cross, and their horses were scrambling onto the bank, dripping as they carried their riders into the village. Warriors and women and many, many curious, frightened children appeared among the few lodges. Ruff-necked, several dogs slinked close to growl at these strange-smelling horses and men—

A single gunshot rang out.

Bird Alighting whirled about on the bare back of that war-horse. In that instant he could not find the warrior who had fired the shot. Nor could he see a one of the soldiers or that Shadow-talker as they fell from their horses.

Then he turned the Looking Glass pony some more and peered across the little river in horror, shocked to find the rest of the Shadows and soldiers speeding their horses down to the water. A gray tendril of gunsmoke was still curling away from the barrel of that bad-talker's rifle!

CHAPTER TEN

JULY 1, 1877

APTAIN STEPHEN G. WHIPPLE JERKED AROUND IN HIS SADDLE AT THE loud boom of the gun, watching as that red-faced, loudmouthed civilian named Washington "Dutch" Holmes entered the stream and slowly lowered the needle-gun from his shoulder, gray smoke snaking from its muzzle.

How in Jupiter had things gotten so out of hand?

For starters, Whipple's detail hadn't been where he had hoped they could be at first light. Because of both the rugged terrain and the miscalculations of Randall's volunteers, the Looking Glass village turned out to be more than ten miles farther than they had assumed when they first embarked from Mount Idaho. After riding through the dark, in broken country, they had ended up on the hillside opposite the village close to 7:00 A.M., well after daybreak.

By then it had become clear some of Randall's men had kept themselves warm, or worked up some bravado, by sipping at a little of the whiskey they passed around in some pewter flasks. Just before Whipple had started into the stream, prepared to parley with Looking Glass, Dutch Holmes's companion Dave Ousterholt had hollered out with a slur, "Tell that red son of a bitch we'll move 'im to Mount Idaho by bullets or bayonets—don't make us no mind!"

The whiskey in their bellies was doing all the talking now, and . . . Katy bar the door!

Just as suddenly as he had jerked around in the saddle to peer at the cursing civilians—Ousterholt and Holmes—the captain now whipped back around to look at the village where most of the Nez Perce stood frozen in place, stunned. Except for that one hapless warrior who had been standing closest on the creek bank. He was clutching both hands around one of his thighs, a dark ooze seeping between his fingers.

Right on the heels of that breathless moment when everything around him seemed to be suspended in time . . . the Indians let out a concerted yell: men with their angry war cries, women with their anguished wails of disbelief, and the children with their fearful, bewildered sobbing. Of a sudden everything was in motion once more, but in a blur now. Women scooped up their children as they dashed behind lodges, seeking safety. Old men stood haranguing the men of fighting age. Warriors sprinted here and there in the bedlam, dashing into their lodges for weapons, reemerging with bows or a few old rifles in hand. Even some young boys leaped bareback atop those horses kept in the village—shrieking as they raced for the herd on the outskirts of camp.

There could be no delay now!

"Retreat!" the captain called to his three fellow soldiers and that single civilian interpreter whom he had brought with him across the creek. "Pull back! Pull back!"

As one the four of them wheeled their horses about, kicking the animals savagely as they leaped off the grassy bank, landing with a spray in the creek running at its full strength with mountain snowmelt. All five riders leaned low across their horses' withers as they raced for the opposite bank where the rest of Whipple's detachment were milling about as they came out of the creek. The first arrows were reaching the far side by the time he and the four were scrambling up the bank to join those two companies of soldiers scattering without orders, seeking cover of any sort.

And in the midst of it all sat those two damned civilians!

"Just what in the name of Jupiter did you think you were doing?" Whipple shouted at the man as he reined up between Dutch Holmes and the rifleman.

"They wasn't gonna do what you wanted 'em to do anyway, Captain," snorted the red-faced, whiskeyed-up Dave Ousterholt. "Lot of useless talk while that Looking Glass and his red bastards have time to get ready to fight."

In fury, Whipple snapped, "We didn't come here to fight!"

The volunteer sneered as he said, "Blood. That's all the red-bellies understand, Captain. Time we give back what they give our friends on the Salmon. For what they done out on the Camas Prairie, too!"

"Damn you! There was no call—"

"You're already in the soup now, Captain," interrupted Dutch Holmes.

"That's right!" Ousterholt said with an evil grin. "Let's take this goddamned village: grab ol' Looking Glass and his boys afore they can put up a fight. You're wasting time jawing with me when there's killing to be done!"

Whipple's horse suddenly sidestepped, fighting the bit, the instant an arrow quivered in its rear flank.

"Fire!" the captain bellowed in frustration—at these two hotheaded civilians and those Indians across the way. "Lay down a covering fire!"

It was only a matter of heartbeats before the men of his battalion began doing just that. Kneeling behind some brush, standing behind trees, crouching behind some low rocks, or sprawled on their bellies—the cavalrymen poured a devastating fire into those warriors streaming toward the creek bank to defend their village. With the fury of their fire, it took no more than the space of four minutes for the Nez Perce to be driven back from the water—back, back toward their lodges.

Behind those few warriors, women and old ones were herding the children over a low hill to the east, scattering out of range from those bullets landing among the buffalo-hide lodges like a spring hailstorm. Every now and again a pony would cry out in pain as a wayward bullet found one of the huge targets.

"Shoot that one getting away!"

Whipple turned, finding Dutch Holmes pointing upstream at a figure wrapped in the hide of a wolf slipping out of the bushes. Several of the civilians instantly trained their weapons on the Indian and fired, forcing the figure to whirl about and retreat into the brush.

As Whipple lunged up on foot, Dave Ousterholt growled at his companions, "Was that a buck or a squaw?"

"Don't fire on the women! That's an order of the U. S. Army!" the captain snarled his answer to the question.

"Them bitches can kill you just as quick as a buck, Captain!" D. B. Randall bellowed in defense of his volunteers. "As for my outfit, we'll shoot anything that moves over there."

"Captain Whipple!"

He turned to find Henry E. Winters racing up, still in the saddle. "We need to get into the village *now!*"

"Agreed, Captain! Deploy your E Troop on a skirmishers' front, right flank. My men will take the left flank—"

Randall interrupted, "What about my volunteers?"

For an instant he considered telling Randall exactly what he could do with his liquored-up, unruly bar brawlers . . . but he reluctantly said, "Spread out behind us and act as reserves." Then Whipple turned quickly so that he wouldn't have to take any more guff from these damnable troublemaking civilians.

Scanning over his L Company, Whipple located First Lieutenant Edwin H. Shelton shaping up the line for their charge. "Mr. Shelton! I want you to pick ten of our men. Get Lieutenant Forse from E Troop to divide off ten of his. Your squad will go after the horse herd. Above everything else, you must surround that herd, prevent it from running off, and capture it."

Shelton snapped a salute. "Capital idea, sir!"

"There must be no failure in your task," Whipple emphasized. "You must get your hands on that herd!"

Wheeling about, Shelton hollered for Lieutenant Albert G. Forse.

It took a few minutes to get the men up and out from behind what cover they had taken, a distressing development to Whipple's way of thinking, since his men weren't suffering any real resistance from the opposite bank at all. Nearly every one of the warriors had taken shelter among the lodges now, making only potshots at best. No concerted defense, nothing of any real danger posed to Whipple's battalion.

The captain was just starting his men off the west bank of the stream—

"I hit the bitch! Whooo-damn! I know I hit her!"

Right by Whipple's elbow, Dave Ousterholt was shouting with unbridled glee, dancing about and pointing as Holmes and Randall pounded him on the back with their congratulations. Just downstream a woman had pitched off her pony, loosing her grip on her infant as she tumbled into the swift water. At the same moment, the frightened horse wheeled around on the uneven, stony stream bottom, the woman and child imprisoned between its flailing legs and slashing hooves. As the pony stumbled, then regained its balance, the woman's head popped to the surface of the swift-flowing stream.

She screamed, slapping the water with her arms, attempting to fight the current, struggling to reach the spot where her child had disappeared beneath the surface. As the pony lurched and lunged across the creek bottom, the woman was tossed about, hurtled downstream away from Whipple's attackers, her faint screams interrupted each time she was bowled over and submerged by the roiling current.

Dutch Holmes cheered his friend, "That's one scalp you can't get your hands on, Dave!"

"Shit!" Ousterholt replied with a wolfish grin. "I brung down two for one bullet! Not bad hunting, I'll wager!"

Whipple finally tore his eyes off the struggling woman as her body was swept around a gentle bend in the creek, carried out of view. He swallowed hard as he whirled around on his heel and roared, "You volunteers—get in and secure the village!"

ALMOST AS SOON as the mean-talker's bullet struck one of the older little chiefs, a man named Shot Leg—who had just returned from the buffalo country only two days before—the soldiers were retreating and Bird Alighting was sucking in another breath. Now all those uniformed *suapies* were diving for cover, where they started to lay down a deadly fire among the eleven poor lodges and those few willow shelters for the young, unmarried warriors.

With a grunt, Shot Leg crumpled to the ground nearby, both hands clamped around his bloody wound. He stared up at Bird Alighting in disbelief. "Can you understand this?" he asked, dazed. "My name is *Tahkoopen*, from a wounding many summers ago—and now I am shot in the same leg again!"

Bird Alighting was just about to cut off a strip of his breechclout when his ears brought him the hammer of hoofbeats. Wheeling about, he saw the two warriors riding up in a blur. Leaping out of the way just in time, he watched as the pair leaned off their mounts and seized hold of the wounded Shot Leg, dragging the warrior away in a blur of color. With him hoisted between them, the horsemen dragged the man toward the eastern hills, where he would be out of danger.

Spinning around, Bird Alighting found himself alone and looking for a pony, any horse that might get him out of the village. Across the creek, the Shadow voices grew louder and more strident. He glanced their way again. They were moving out of cover, advancing on the bank—preparing to cross. Around him the bullets slapped the thick buffalo hides now, chipped splinters off the lodgepoles. Whined like angry wasps as the air grew deadly around him and the frightened, wandering cattle bawled helplessly, stirring dust as if in a buffalo surround. The odor of fresh manure and urine from the ponies and beeves stung his nostrils—

There—he saw a pony!

It was struggling against its long halter rope, lashed to a stake at the side of a lodge. Forgotten and forsaken by its owner already run into the hills.

Imene kaizi yeu yeu, Hunyewat! he mouthed his thankful praise to the Creator as he burst into a sprint, racing for the pony bucking and rearing near the middle of the small camp.

Seizing hold of the long halter, Bird Alighting was nearly yanked off his feet by the powerful animal before he looped the rope around one wrist and freed the knot with his other hand. Wild-eyed with terror, the pony watched as the man lunged past its neck and leaped onto the narrow back.

Drawing up the excess rope, Bird Alighting suddenly realized something was wrong. The horse stood perfectly still, as if turned into stone.

"Amtiz! Ueye!" he shouted into the horse's ear, slapping its front and rear flank with that coil of rope. "Let's go! Run!"

It was as if the ground exploded beneath him when the pony started bucking. Interlacing his fingers within its mane, locking his toes beneath its belly, gripping that rope with all his strength, Bird Alighting bounced into the air, landing on the horse's bare back with a brutal thud each time the animal struck the ground.

As the pony whipped itself into a whirling dance, Bird Alighting spotted the *suapies* and the other Shadows reaching the middle of the stream, their horses threading through the strong current, all but having reached the near bank.

His horse landed again with a teeth-jarring thud, then trembled and stood still once more—

A burning ribbon of fire licked through his thigh.

Bird Alighting jerked from the pain, his eyes finding the soldiers on the near bank and beginning to urge their dripping horses in among the lodges. The muzzles of their weapons were smoking. And he knew he had been hit by one of their bullets.

"Mimillu!" he screeched at the horse, knowing this was his only chance to flee. "You stupid creature!"

In his gut, Bird Alighting realized he would never stand a chance on foot, not with that wounded leg burning. He'd never manage to put any weight on that side of his body in a run to escape.

Whipping the pony with the coil of rope on one side, flailing his one good foot against the other side, the warrior finally got the horse started away through the lodges. But slowly. The animal took a few tentative steps, paused and whipped its head around, then set off again at a little faster pace.

Not far ahead Bird Alighting saw another man running in the same direction, for the base of the hill where the women and children had disappeared. One bullet, then a handful more, snarled past him and the horse as the warrior on foot peered over his shoulder and spotted Bird Alighting coming.

With those oncoming *suapies* and the Shadows, Bird Alighting realized death would not be long in finding the man left to flee on foot. He would be run down—shot from behind or clubbed with a rifle before he was finished off at close range.

"Come up behind me!" he shouted to the warrior as he drew near.

Without a word, the breathless warrior lurched to a halt and held up his hand. Grabbing it in his, Bird Alighting swung the man up behind him on the slow horse.

That exertion suddenly seemed to fill the morning sky with shooting stars. He found it hard to focus, could not see much of anything at all around him as he began to wobble on the back of the pony.

"Hold on! Hold on!" the warrior behind him yelled in his ear.

But Bird Alighting was having trouble staying upright. He wanted to tell the man about his leg wound, that he must be losing too much blood, that his head was not working right anymore and he could not see. . . .

Then all color, all light, went out of his body—

RACING OUT OF the north and east sides of the village, more than a hundred of the Nez Perce were streaming away from Captain Whipple's troops and D. B. Randall's Mount Idaho volunteers.

They reminded Lieutenant Sevier M. Rains of rats streaming from the tall piles of grain sacks rising from the wharves in Lewiston. Why, if Whipple ordered these eighty-some men after the Indians, it would be like trying to contain mercury under their fingers. A worse than useless proposition. Little more than a fool's errand.

"Mr. Rains!"

He wheeled his horse at Whipple's call, found the officer approaching on horseback. "Captain?"

"You're to be commended, Lieutenant," Whipple began, a bit breathless.

"Commended, Captain?"

"Racing ahead of the skirmish line the way you did—alone."

"Truth is, sir . . . I was hoping to catch Looking Glass myself. I figured he was the biggest prize of all. But I think he got away with the rest."

"Next to that chief, their horses are the next biggest prize we could hope to corral," Whipple advised. "With two of my lieutenants gone after the herd, I need you to take charge of the destruction of the camp."

"Burn the lodges, sir?"

"Yes. See how the volunteers are already going through every one—looting all that is worth a pittance."

"Firearms, powder, that sort of thing, Captain?"

"Save it from the fires, but torch the rest."

Rains touched his fingertips to his brow in salute. "Very good, Captain!"

As it turned out, the lieutenant's detail could get no more than two of the lodges burning. The hides were either too damp to burn with the morning dew or simply too thick to do more than smolder. For the better part of an hour it was like a celebration for Randall's civilians as they hooped and hollered each time one of them dragged something of value from the captured lodges. Small buckskin pouches of black powder, satchels of vermillion paint, and finely tanned buffalo robes, not to mention cooking utensils, blankets, china dishes, and some clayware. Anything that could not be set ablaze was stomped on or busted with the butt of their rifles, broken in pieces so small no one would waste time retrieving them from the damp ground.

"Hey, Lieutenant!" D. B. Randall called out to Rains as the officer came to a halt by a lodge standing at the edge of camp. "You see how my friend Minturn proved himself the best shot of this whole bunch, didn'cha?"

"Can't say as I had an eye on any of your men in particular, Mr. Randall."

"Shit, Lieutenant!" Randall exclaimed, waving over one of his fellow civilians. "Here, this is Peter Minturn—best shot in this here territory, I'll wager."

Rains glanced quickly at the young volunteer's face, saw the bemused pride in Minturn's eyes. He asked the volunteer, "So you accounted for some enemy dead, did you?"

Instead of Minturn answering for himself, Randall snorted, "Hell, Lieutenant—this here friend of mine was hungry for Injun meat, I'll tell you. The man damn well proved himself to be a dead shot each time he pulled the trigger!"

"H-hungry for Indian meat?" Rains repeated, bewildered by the crude expression.

Minturn finally spoke: "Just like I'm off hunting to make meat for the stew pot, Lieutenant. This here jump on Looking Glass's village was no different than shooting into a bunch of scampering jackrabbits!"

CHAPTER ELEVEN

Khoy-Tsahl, 1877

LOWLY, GROGGILY, BIRD ALIGHTING CAME ALIVE AGAIN.
He looked around. Felt the arms locked about him. Stared down at those two hands wrapped in the horse's mane and wondered whose they were.

Then all color and light returned to his mind—and he remembered the warrior he had stopped to pick up in his flight from the village.

Sensing the labored, uneven lope of the overburdened horse, Bird Alighting gazed down at his legging, finding half of it entirely soaked with his blood. Even though he was still light-headed, the warrior realized he had suffered a severe loss of blood and hadn't fallen for only one reason—the man behind him.

"See our friend?" the warrior behind him yelled in his ear. "She's coming out to us!"

Bewildered, Bird Alighting looked in the direction of the approaching hoofbeats—his eyes finding *Etemiere* coming off the hillside at a gallop. This woman, called Arrowhead among his *Nee-Me-Poo*, was racing toward them at a slant out of the skimpy timber. She had a large gray-black wolfskin tied around her neck, its head positioned atop hers, held in place by a cord knotted under her chin. With the speed of her pony, that drape fluttered behind her as she slowed to a lope, coming alongside them and matching the pace of their pony.

"I tried to find a place in the brush at the creek's edge where I could make some shots at the *suapies*," she said breathlessly. "Make some kills across the water—" but Arrowhead suddenly interrupted her words when her eyes saw Bird Alighting's wound. "You are bleeding—badly! Stop—stop your horse now!"

The warrior behind him pulled with one hand in the pony's mane, the other tugging on that long coil of rope Bird Alighting still gripped in one palm, convincing the frightened pony to stop. Immediately vaulting from her horse, Arrowhead leaned over, pulling up the bottom of her cloth dress with one hand as she yanked a knife from its belt scabbard with her other and quickly hacked off two long strips of the wool cloth.

Standing at Bird Alighting's knee, Arrowhead quickly folded one piece over the seeping wound, then flung the other, wider strip around the leg itself. She pulled her makeshift bandage as tight as she could before looping the ends into a knot, then secured it with a second knot. "Perhaps this will stop the bleeding now."

"Yes," the warrior behind him agreed quietly. "Then his mind won't go to sleep again from losing any more blood. But we will need to get him some raw liver to eat soon."

All Bird Alighting could do was nod. Eating raw liver was the best thing for the weakness caused from a great loss of blood.

"I saw a young herder boy killed," Arrowhead told them as she inspected the bandage she had just tied around the leg. "He was trying to drive off the horses when the Shadows came charging up to steal the herd from us."

"You saw him fall?"

"Yes. He pitched off the back of his pony and did not move," she explained. "I wanted to go see to him, if there was any breath left in his mouth—but the herding ground was too crowded with soldiers by that time. They were shooting at me, so I hurried to the hills to catch up with the rest of our village."

"What will we do now?" the warrior asked as Arrowhead turned away to leap atop her pony.

She said, "We should find the rest of our people."

A crackle of sporadic gunfire sounded dangerously close as they gave heels to their ponies and started toward the top of the hill.

With desperation in his voice, the warrior declared, "No, I mean to ask: What will Looking Glass's people do now that we have lost all our horses, left our lodges and homes and gardens behind . . . abandoned everything we own?"

"What law of warfare says an enemy has the right to shoot you when you are surrendering?" Bird Alighting asked, surprising them both that he was talking after so long a silence.

"It is evil treachery," the warrior growled. "To shoot at innocents."

"There is only one thing we can do," Bird Alighting added, the colors in his mind more crisp and certain than they ever had been. "Blood will always follow blood."

"Is your head right, Bird Alighting? Or is your thinking gone far away?" asked Arrowhead. "What do you mean—blood will always follow blood?"

In a stronger voice, he said, "Now is the time we must join the rest of Looking Glass's people and go in search of the others who are fighting these Shadows and soldiers."

SECOND LIEUTENANT SEVIER M. Rains had done an admirable job plundering the village . . . even if he did say so himself. His father had ransacked Seminole villages in Florida, Mexican towns far south of the border, then struggled in a lost cause against Federal troops during the Civil War. He would approve of the way the lieutenant and his men left nothing of any value for the Nez Perce.

"Lieutenant!" Captain Whipple called out as he approached with Captain Winters.

"Sir!" and Rains snapped a salute as the officers' eyes raked over the destruction he had made of Looking Glass's camp.

Whipple asked, "Are you far from completing your assignment?"

"We are all but finished, Captain."

"Good," Winters said. "We're about to move out."

"Where to, sirs?" Rains inquired.

"Back toward Mount Idaho," Whipple explained. "We're going to give more than six hundred horses to the volunteers, hoping to keep them out of the hands of the hostiles. Then we'll rejoin our column across the Salmon."

Winters added, "General Howard should have the command across the river by now."

"So we're going to join in the pursuit?" Rains asked after he had given the command for his detail to mount up.

"This bunch won't cause any more trouble, I'd wager," Winters snorted.

Whipple agreed as he gestured for them to move out, starting upstream. "With what little we're leaving behind for his band, we've taken Looking Glass entirely out of the equation for the rest of the war, gentlemen."

Rains still felt the hot giddiness that had come from the brief fight forcing their way into the enemy camp. "I sure hope we're *not* done, sirs."

"What do you mean, Mr. Rains?" Whipple asked.

"I only hope the general will leave some warriors for us," Rains admitted. "I pray we're not too late to get in on a little more fighting before this shabby, second-rate war is over."

AFTER SENDING A courier upriver to remind Captain Joel G. Trimble to hurry across the Salmon and rejoin the column, General O. O. Howard could now begin his tortuous pursuit of the Non-Treaty bands as the warriors and their families slipped away into the wrinkles of that rugged terrain rising steeply between the Salmon and Snake Rivers.

Back on their first night in Camp Theller at Horseshoe Bend in the Salmon, William Hunter and more than forty of his volunteers had arrived in camp. They had announced they were from Dayton, in Washington Territory—a small town midway between Lewiston and Walla Walla—come to help the general put down the uprising in any fashion they could. Howard had put them to work early the next morning, 29 June. Hunter himself and a pair of his civilians willingly stripped off their clothes, dragged the saddles from their horses, then braved the icy-cold, roiling torrent of the Salmon as they dragged two lengths of thick rope and their pulleys to the west bank. Reaching the far side, they dismounted to the raucous cheers of Howard's hundreds. With three rowboats acquired from settlers living upstream, the long column could now begin its crossing and its pursuit of Joseph's Non-Treaty bands, one boatload of soldiers at a time.

The goal was to attach a boat to the main cable by means of a loop sling, muscling each small load back and forth with the muscles of their backs pitted against the strength of the Salmon. But the ropes Hunter's men lashed to a trio of stout, stately cottonwoods did not last out the day's battering and buffeting as Howard started his command across. What with the strength of a snow-swollen current, the hemp lines finally gave out early in the afternoon, and one of the hastily constructed rafts started spinning downriver with its terrified crew. Almost a mile down the Salmon, they managed to beach their unwieldy craft and step onto solid ground.

The following day, 30 June, the soldiers attempted something stronger in the way of a wire cable, hoping it would prove stronger than the rope . . . but it, too, ultimately failed against the racing current. With less than half the men having reached the west bank, most still on the east side with the general, this second day ended in even more frustration for Howard.

Contrary to those who would eventually claim that he was overpious and refused to march on Sundays, O. O. Howard himself crossed the Salmon on the afternoon of 1 July after holding a small prayer service for his officers and what enlisted men chose to attend. It was a miserable day, raining and snowing alternately, as the general followed William Hunter and four of his men into the Salmon River breaks—where they nonetheless did find half a thousand Nez Perce ponies they managed to herd back to the crossing and forced across the river. Those animals that did not drown in the turbulent waters were turned over to Lieutenant James A. Haughey and his H Company of the Twenty-first Infantry, called up from Fort Vancouver. While the rest of the command had boated to the west side of the river, Haughey's detail remained on the east bank to guard Howard's supply depot.

It was no small victory, therefore, that by sundown of 1 July the general had removed 500 ponies from his enemy and his entire column was finally across the frothy Salmon—in addition to their pack train, ammunition and supplies, artillery pieces, and other assorted impedimenta. An intermittent rain continued to fall, swelling the river at their backs, turning the green hills around them into a slick, soggy quagmire.

With no time to celebrate their victory over the Salmon, Howard's column now had to face another, and perhaps even more daunting, ordeal.

For the three days before he had reached Horseshoe Bend with his command, it had rained off and on. But once they were in Camp Theller beside the Salmon, the skies were gutted and it began to pour almost nonstop, a storm that lasted three more days and nights while the soldiers struggled to get their animals and matériel across the Salmon. What part of the trail hadn't been turned into a sticky morass had become so slick that even the surefooted mules were having difficulty maintaining their grip on the mushy hillsides.

The packers who handled those mules hadn't hired on to accept army scrip or paper greenbacks in exchange for their ordeal. Instead, the civilians were to be paid the going rate of one dollar per animal, per day, in "coin," or what those grizzled frontiersmen called hard money. But that was just for the use, and steady abuse, of their animals. The packers themselves were paid even more. Howard had engaged ten of the best mule-skinners in the country at eighty-five dollars in coin per month and another forty-eight packers for sixty-five dollars in hard money.

But securing enough money for their pay was the least of Howard's problems. He had other, niggling details that bellowed for his attention. For one thing, his quartermasters had assured themselves that all their supply wagons had the proper number of wheels before setting out from Fort Lapwai. A shipment of dead-axle (or springless) wagons was brought upriver from Portland by the Oregon Steam Navigation Company. Problem was, the riverboat company hadn't brought wagons up with two *front* wheels and two *rear* wheels! Then, too, much of the harness supplied Howard's teamsters was already dried and rotten as unscrupulous traders attempted to make their quick money off this brief action against the Nez Perce.

But when he got a wagon with the correct complement of wheels and hitched up the teams with usable, field-worthy harness . . . Howard found he still wasn't able to hire enough teamsters from the surrounding countryside. Most of the low-end laboring classes in the Idaho towns were already attached to the column to help as road-building crews, who were paid a skimpy daily wage and found. Still, many of the teamsters he was able to hire out of the towns ended up quitting once the army crossed the Salmon and the going toughened far beyond what any of them had bargained for.

Most of the hangers-on, those so-called volunteers, with their leaders brandishing honorary titles, had already become an inconstant irritation to the general as well. The first bunch, twenty-one citizens from Walla Walla under Tom Page who had accompanied Howard to the battlefield days ago, ended up quitting and turning around for home, citing "pressing business," before Howard even had his column across the Salmon! Fortunate for the general and his campaign, that very same day William Hunter and his forty men had showed up from Dayton.

But a third cadre of some twenty-five citizens under "Captain" J. W. Elliott were a different color of horse altogether. They had reported in, then promptly rode off, creating more of a nuisance of themselves in the area than they were assisting the army in putting down this rebellion. That band of volunteers from Pomeroy, a small community some twenty-five miles east of Dayton in Washington Territory, had disgusted Howard in that they were far more interested in rustling any local settler's loose stock than in pursuing the Non-Treaty Nez Perce.

And it wasn't only the civilians in this area who seemed to be securely resting at the bottom of the proverbial barrel. Major General Irwin McDowell, commander of the Division of the Pacific and Howard's superior, was scraping the bottom of his own barrel when he ordered C Company of the Twelfth Infantry up from Fort Yuma in Arizona, including its own junior officer, Second Lieutenant Guy Howard—the general's oldest son. Upon his arrival, Otis would make Guy one of his aides for the duration of the Nez Perce conflict. In addition, McDowell ordered up the Eighth Infantry's H Company, then in California. By the time those two outfits reached San Francisco by train, McDowell had added companies C and L from the Fourth Artillery. Altogether, that was a complement of ninety-six unproven, untested soldiers and ten officers. Together with thirty-two green recruits fresh from their enlistment depots back east, all were loaded onto a steamer and sent north to Portland. They reached Lewiston on 19 June, the quickest deployment for any troop shipment then under way.

All the delays and those men pouring in from around the country reminded O. O. Howard of that most unholy of holdovers from their days fighting the Civil War when the highest echelons of the Union command refused to budge, much less engage the Confederates, until they were assured of superior numbers and thereby certain of victory even before they marched into battle.

In order to track the Non-Treaty bands, Howard realized he needed a complement of trustworthy scouts. While it was not near the number Howard had requested, McDowell nonetheless authorized the hiring of twenty-five Indian trackers. Later, on the fifth of July, Howard would be instructed that he could hire a total of eighty in all—some of which came from Fort Hall on the Bannock-Shoshone Reservation, a number of those having seen service in the previous year's campaign against the Sioux and Cheyenne on the Northern Plains. With his supply line assured, his manpower being hustled to the front, and competent guides mustered to keep him on the Nez Perce's trail, Howard felt assured of putting an early end to this outbreak.

Still, the delays and lack of rapid progress had been frustrating to the old soldier.

The fleeing bands had chosen well when they crossed into this forbidding landscape of a rugged and lofty terrain squeezed up between the two deep, precipitous, and all-but-inaccessible canyons of the Salmon and Snake Rivers, just south of the point where the Salmon angled west in its quest to join the Snake. Atop the ridges lay a broken undulating prairie, while the only route to that plateau forced a horseman up the steep walls of the Salmon River gorge. Those slopes were a mixture of grassy prairie dotted with patches of evergreen timber.*

Because the column was taxed in its climb to ever-higher altitudes, the excruciating exertion on man and animal began to show. While every soldier had his own complaints, the artillerymen grumbled the loudest. After Captain Charles B. Throckmorton, commander of the artillery battalion, had shown himself to be a laggard by the time they reached the Salmon, Howard had replaced him with Captain Marcus P. Miller. After only two days the fact that the artillerymen were unused to Indian campaigning was painfully apparent. Miller's four gun crews let it be known what a toll it was taking on them as they struggled to keep up with the cavalry and infantry companies.

It wasn't that Howard's scouts had trouble finding and following the Non-Treaty bands—what with Joseph's people cutting a wide, telltale swath as more than seven hundred people drove along more than two thousand horses, many dragging travois. But at times the command

---

*Much of this area crossed by both the Nez Perce and Howard's army in 1877 is today known as the Joseph Plains.

reached a short stretch of that well-marked trail where the passage proved so slippery, the footing so treacherous, that a few of the pack animals slid right over the edge, tumbling down and down until some trees or jagged rocks put an end to their descent hundreds of yards below. By the time packers scrambled back down to see what they could salvage, there wasn't much left of either the loose-footed mules or what supplies the animals had been carrying.

Able to advance rarely more than ten, perhaps as much as twelve, miles per day, Howard cajoled, begged, and snapped at his column to keep them after their prey. Meanwhile, his scouts could only prod the soldiers with the distressing news that the Non-Treaty bands were staying far, far in the lead.

No surprise, it continued to rain as they struggled toward the summit of Brown's Mountain. But as they made that grueling 3,500-foot ascent, the rain turned to snow. Just below the summit, the entire command had to halt and hunker down as the wind came up, the clouds pressed down, and they were battered by a freezing sleet that soaked every man, caked every animal, in layers of bone-chilling ice. During the storm that night, the cooks attempted to prepare a dish made from abandoned and broken-down Nez Perce horses, which, among the officers, was laughingly called *fricandeau de cheval*. Most claimed it tasted like a stringy beef, so the majority opted for their ration of salt pork as they hunkered around their blazing fires, the wind howling through what some now labeled Camp Misery.

By the time Howard reached the summit, he had convinced himself that Joseph's people had split into two bands. To meet the threat posed by the one group he was certain was inching its way south to unite with the dissident Shoshone and Bannock tribes along the Weiser River, the general had already ordered that troops under Major John Wesley Green march north from Fort Boise to the seat of the Indian war—thereby trapping the Nez Perce between them.

But what of the other, larger group?

Otis believed they still marched in front of him—that he could follow them until he caught them in camp, immediately surround them, and force a surrender. He became even more certain of this scenario when his Nez Perce scouts located one cache after another, each containing some of what the Non-Treaty warriors had stolen from the homes of the Salmon River and Camas Prairie settlers: cigars and clothing, flour and meerschaum pipes, along with other sundry supplies. The afternoon of their third day west of the Salmon, the advance even ran onto more than five hundred horses that had evidently strayed off from the Nez Perce herd.

Destroying the cached supplies and ordering the horses driven back across the river, Howard convinced himself that all this circumstantial evidence indicated that Joseph was leading his people back toward the Wallowa and Imnaha valleys—the chief's traditional camping grounds.

While his officers grumbled among themselves, while the bone-weary, soaked-clear-through soldiers glared at their commander, Oliver Otis Howard steadfastly assured himself that he was about to bring the war to an end.

Joseph was taking his bands back to their ancestral homes, where they would be trapped between two converging armies. It was only a matter of time now, Howard vowed. A few more days and a few more miles.

This damnable little war was almost over.

CHAPTER TWELVE

JULY 2, 1877

I CAN'T ORDER YOU TO STAY ON THIS SIDE OF THE RIVER, MR. HUNTER," GEN-eral O. O. Howard had told the civilian leader from Dayton back on that first day the soldiers were attempting their perilous crossing. "Nor can I guarantee your safety if you go wandering off alone on the other side of the Salmon."

"You still have your mind set against sending any of your friendlies out to find the war camp, General?" asked William Hunter.

"Not until I have enough of my men across should we have any more dis-plays from the warriors like we had here day before yesterday."

"Mind you, me and my men don't aim to get ourselves in any trouble, General Howard," the civilian had assured him. "Just want to see where those Nez Perce have run off to. We figure to be back before this time tomorrow."

He and two of his best friends from Dayton—a tiny community in east-ern Washington Territory—swam their horses over to the west bank of the Salmon, then started north into the broken country. They hadn't been mov-ing more than two hours when they were rewarded with sighting a half-dozen figures on foot in the distance.

"*Enfant de garce!*" one of the six men sobbed as they lunged up among the trio of horsemen.

"Shit, any of you Americans?" Hunter asked, perplexed. "Speak Eng-lish?"

"A little some," confessed another of the bedraggled half-dozen.

"You look a sight, fellas," Hunter said. "Where's your horses? Your guns?"

The good-talker shook his head as if searching for the right words, per-haps any words, to use in telling the story as Hunter and his companions dropped to the ground and let their horses blow. Slowly, painstakingly, the story unfolded.

When the outbreak first began, the six Frenchmen had been on this west side of the Salmon, farther to the south. In fact, they claimed they had yelled a warning across the river to some American friends. Once hundreds of the Nez Perce showed up near the mouth of the White Bird, the Frenchmen fled deep into the hills on the other side of the Salmon. But not so far they hadn't heard all the gunfire the day of the battle.

Keeping to their side of the river, they had trained a keen eye on the migrations of the Non-Treaty bands as the Indians moved south to Horse-shoe Bend, then crossed and started back north to where Larry Ott had been homesteading on Deer Creek then started to climb into the formidable terrain. Three days ago they had run across a trio of Chinese miners who warned them that war parties were prowling the countryside, horsemen who had allowed the Chinese to pass unharmed.

Two days back, the Frenchmen had taken refuge, hiding in a tiny abandoned cabin when they heard horses approaching outside, and were suddenly confronted with five warriors armed with rifles. The frightened Frenchmen quickly surrendered their three old shotguns. Before they rode off, the Nez Perce took more than one hundred dollars in gold and coin from the six miners—then told the Frenchmen to get away as far and as fast as they could from the country where no white man would be safe.

William Hunter dragged the short stub of his fat stogie from his teeth and thoughtfully inspected the moist, much-chewed end of the cigar. Then he said, "Lost your bird guns to them red bastards, and all your money, too."

"They say they give us our lives in trade," the French miner repeated.

"Tell you what, fellas," Hunter declared. "You talk it over together, because I'll guarantee you boys one thing: If you throw in with us and Howard's soldiers . . . you won't just get back what guns and money is owed you, but a whole heap of revenge, too."

WHILE THE *SUAPIES* of Cut-Off Arm were struggling to maintain any momentum at all, the Non-Treaty bands were already more than twenty miles downstream, north along the Salmon at a traditional fording site known as Craig Billy Crossing. Joseph realized they had chosen well when they decided to follow the suggestions of Rainbow and Five Wounds, just returned from the buffalo country the afternoon of the fight at *Lahmotta*.

"We cross the Salmon, wait for the soldiers to follow, then lose them on the other side," Rainbow had advised.

"And when we have lured the Shadows across, getting them snarled and lost in that rugged country, we will recross," Five Wounds proposed. "That's when we'll be free to roam as we always have."

Days ago, the scouts watched two smaller groups of soldiers leave Cut-Off Arm's massed army. One band took its empty pack animals and marched north for Fort Lapwai, clearly intending to bring back more supplies—which meant a longer effort on their part. An army so large surely needed a great deal of food. But that second band of *suapies* had marched directly for the settlements of Grangeville and Mount Idaho with a wagon gun, and from there they moved at night into the twisting canyon of the Clearwater, where the scouts lost track of the soldiers. None of the *Nee-Me-Poo* warrior chiefs could figure out where the *suapies* were bound or why.

After three days of struggle, Cut-Off Arm's foolish soldiers made it across the river—which meant it was finally time for the village to break camp where they had been waiting just north of the crossing, near the Deer Creek homestead of Larry Ott,[*] where there was a little level ground on which to

---

[*]*Cries from the Earth*, vol. 14, the *Plainsmen* series.

pitch their lodges against the rainy sky. Now they must forge their way across the muddy, broken landscape, climbing toward the Doumecq Plain above that evil Shadow's abandoned farm.

But to make time and to assure that they would stay far enough ahead of the soldiers, they would not be able to take everything from this point. As the chief in charge of the women and children, overseeing the camp itself, Joseph ordered that every unnecessary item of food and clothing be buried in numerous caches dug near rocks they would mark for their return when the present troubles were over.

And then he had turned to the young men not yet old enough to have fought against the soldiers at *Lahmotta*, youngsters nonetheless old enough to experience an eager enthusiasm. Their orders were to cull the old and the lame horses from their combined herds. These animals would be separated out from the stronger horses, then driven down their back trail where they would likely encounter the slowly advancing soldiers at some point in the next few days. It was a maneuver that might not necessarily retard the progress of the *suapies* but most assuredly would accelerate the progress of the camp in its march.

In the two weeks since his brother had defeated the horse soldiers at *Lahmotta*, there had been much said about Joseph behind the chief's back. None of it was good. Nearly all the talk was about his not taking up a weapon to fight off the soldiers, how he had not ventured out of camp to do battle even though Ollokot's warriors were outnumbered two-to-one. For some time now the talk whispered and often laughed about behind the hands had not been good.

But it was in these last few days that Joseph began to establish the reputation that would withstand the test yet to come. A legacy that would endure those terrible trials the *Nee-Me-Poo* could not even imagine at that moment. It was in this time that Joseph began to make decisions not having anything whatsoever to do with making war on some group of Shadow civilians or on that band of soldiers. No, without the showy fanfare of the war chiefs, Joseph had already begun to quietly reach decisions that—months from now and many, many miles away—would ultimately assure the survival of his people.

There was no country better suited to ducking and dodging than this between the Snake and Salmon Rivers. And while Cut-Off Arm got bogged down in the mire of crags and rain-slickened trails, the *Nee-Me-Poo* would leap back across the Salmon, across the Camas Prairie, and on to the deep canyon of the Cottonwood that would lead the bands all the way to the Clearwater. Because this hard country lay in an arduous maze, few of the individual family groups or clans wandered away on their own. Fear of what followed them bound the many together and kept them moving north.

At one point they came across a large herd of cattle that Joseph's *Wallamwatkins* had been forced to abandon weeks ago when they crossed the Salmon at Rocky Canyon to join the last ever of the celebrations at *Tepahlewam*—just before the first settlers were murdered. After stopping here for most of a day, just long enough to butcher a few of the cattle, the village pushed on, leaving the lion's share of the beeves behind in the hills to graze until a better day when Joseph's people hoped to return here, when they could gather up their herd to take it back to their beloved Wallowa valley. But at this point in their flight they could ill afford the snail's pace burden of the white man's beef.

"*Eeh!* Look below!" one of the riders near the front of the march hollered out in unbounded joy.

Joseph smiled at his wife, then put heels to his pony as he sped along the column. Reining up beside Ollokot and Yellow Wolf, he gazed down the steep slope of the canyon.

"Our ford across the *Tahmonah,** Brother," Ollokot announced as they paused to gaze down at their traditional crossing.**

"Now that we've left Cut-Off Arm behind to struggle through these mountains," Joseph said quietly, "we can start across the prairie, where we'll rejoin Looking Glass's people."

"Once we reach that valley of the Clearwater," Ollokot agreed, "the soldiers won't know where to find us. And if they do come looking for our camps, the dark canyons east of *Kamisnim Takin*† are good places for our people to hide. Cut-Off Arm will never find us there."

AS FOR HIS own wound, Bird Alighting counted himself fortunate.

It could have been far, far worse for the rest of Looking Glass's band. Good that the Shadows were such poor shots when they became excited or angry or frightened. All those soldiers and the Shadows had managed to shoot only one *Nee-Me-Poo*, the young pony herder—named *Nennin Chekoostin*, called Black Raven—who had been caught in some cross fire before he could escape as their horse herd was captured. The other two deaths the enemy had caused only because of the terror the Shadows had created when they opened fire, without warning, on the sleepy morning camp. That young woman and her little infant—both of them drowned in Clear Creek—their bodies unclaimed until the white men left and the Looking Glass people could slip back into their devastated camp to look for what they could salvage.

A few of the women and one old man burned their hands putting out the smoldering fires of those two lodges the *suapies* had managed to destroy, hoping to save anything that hadn't yet burned. Oh, there were a few scrapes and cuts from running through the brush or stumbling among the rocks as the men, women, and children scrambled out of camp, fleeing beyond the hill just behind the village.

While the sun went down and the stars came out that day, Looking Glass and what warriors hadn't already gone off to join White Bird's and *Toohool-hoolzote*'s fighting men gathered in the descending darkness and talked of

---

*The Salmon River.
**While the white men would come to know this as Craig Billy Crossing, to the *Nee-Me-Poo* this was "Luke's Place," named after *Pahka Yatwekin*, one of their people who was called Luke Billy by the Shadows, a man who had a poor cabin standing on the south bank of the Salmon River.
†The Camas Prairie.

what to do and where to go now that Cut-Off Arm had made war on them. It had served no purpose for their chief to stay neutral, many argued. The white man had attacked them. Even a neighboring chief camped nearby, the Palouse *Hatalekin*, was as homeless as they. Now they must choose.

"Even though we are already on the reservation," Looking Glass protested, "our feet must take one path or another from this moment on."

"We must drive the *suapies* from our country!" shouted Arrowhead, the warrior woman.

"The enemy will keep looking for our camps, which means the women and children will continue to suffer," argued *Hatalekin*, the Palouse chief. "See how the soldiers came looking to attack White Bird."

Shot Leg laughed and said, "But see what good it did those soldiers!"

"Yet other soldiers came looking for another village to attack, and this time it was ours!" Black Foot continued the lament.

"There really is little choice," Looking Glass interrupted the heated discussion minutes later. "Do we want to become Christian Indians like Lawyer's or Reuben's people?"

"No!" Arrowhead growled throatily. "*Tananisa!* Damn them! Let the Kamiah people believe in the white man's god. We are Dreamers!"

"Or," Looking Glass continued, "do we join the fight to hold onto this land of ours?"

"As for me," Black Foot said, "there is no choice in what options the Shadows have handed us."

Slowly the chief looked over that suddenly hushed gathering. A small child whimpered from the dark. Then it was quiet, so deathly quiet, again. The summer night held its breath around them.

When he finally spoke again, Looking Glass said, "We will leave as soon as our women have everything packed on what horses we managed to save from the enemy."

"Where is it you would have us go?" *Hatalekin* asked as the black of night seemed to swallow all their hopes of staying neutral in the struggle.

"We will go in search of the fighting bands," the chief answered. "Our only strength now lies in fighting the white man together."

The moon had just made its appearance at the horizon, its creamy yellow color illuminating the underbellies of some scattered clouds by the time Looking Glass and two old men started the village downstream for the Clearwater. From there they would strike upstream for the mouth of the Cottonwood. It was that creek and its canyon they would follow up and onto the Camas Prairie in the dark of this night.

How noiseless they made that march. The children who had been wrapped in arms or carried on backs had surely fallen asleep. No one talked but some headmen who spoke in low voices of hearing reports of the few warriors who rode both flanks, out there in the dark. From time to time Bird Alighting and the other young men came in to report their news on what lay ahead upon the route Looking Glass had chosen for them all.

In the first, early light of the sun's coming Bird Alighting saw the smudge along the western horizon of the prairie. He rubbed his eyes again, blinked, and stared. He had never been one of those far-seeing men who had the ability to find distant objects without the far-seeing glasses of the Shadows. So he did his best to determine what the smudge meant.

"Is that dust?" Arrowhead asked in almost a whisper as she rode up and came to a halt beside Bird Alighting.

"I cannot tell if it is dust . . . or maybe smoke."

The warrior woman asked, "Where is it? Can you tell that?"

"Far up Cottonwood Creek," Bird Alighting said. "Perhaps as far away as that Shadow settlement on the road to the soldier fort."

"I think it is dust," Arrowhead asserted. "That much dust . . . cannot be Cut-Off Arm's *suapies*. He has his army far to the south of here. No, Bird Alighting, that can only be some of our own people."

How he wanted to smile, his heart wanted to hope. But his head would not let him. "Let's hope your eyes are right, *Etemiere*. I pray those are not soldiers barring our way."

CHAPTER THIRTEEN

I T HADN'T TAKEN VERY LONG FOR FIRST SERGEANT MICHAEL MCCARTHY TO figure out that Trimble's H Company should have stayed at Slate Creek with the civilians huddled there. Far, far better than what they had been forced to endure as they slogged along after those damned fleeing Indians.

From downriver at the crossing General Howard sent orders by "Colonel" Edward McConville and his Mount Idaho volunteers that Captain Trimble's outfit was to rejoin him on the west side of the Salmon. In company with that band of volunteers, they had made their own crossing right there at the mouth of Slate Creek in a driving rain, then marched down the west bank until they reached a house said to belong to a Mr. Rhett. While Trimble's horse soldiers began to take cover out of the soggy weather, Rhett showed up and angrily ordered the men out of his cozy cabin. McConville's men shared their meager canvas shelters with the cavalrymen that stormy night of 1 July.

"Not a good goddamned reception from one of our own citizens!" McCarthy grumbled, wishing he could pry the wet boots off his feet.

"Sorry that son of a bitch ain't got a touch of hospitality in his soul," McConville apologized. "Some folks don't give a damn what the army's here to do for 'em."

Ascending Deer Creek the next morning, Captain Trimble had started them into the rugged hills, following the route taken by the fleeing Nez Perce.

A perfect sea of mountains, gullies, ravines, and canyons.

Each day's march of ten miles seemed more like a march three times as far made on level ground. What had been merely difficult terrain before the incessant rains had now become treacherous as the slopes turned into rivers of mud. With the cavalry assigned to lead the way, that first afternoon they had reached the top of a small plateau just at dusk, turning in their saddles to peer back at that long line slowly snaking its way up the precipitous mountainside. Trimble ordered a bivouac made near some stunted pines, and the men did what they could to make it a cheerful camp. Still, most everything, tents and rations included, was back with the pack train and infantry, neither of which would likely catch up to the advance until midday tomorrow. So all these troopers had was what little coffee, hardbread, and bacon remained in their saddlebags.

To add to the misery of their bivouac at the summit of Brown's Mountain on the evening of 2 July, a cheerless camp made in the open without much in the way of supper, just after dark a hard and icy rain began lancing out of the sky. Most of the officers ended up crowding into the general's headquarters tent, leaving the noncoms and enlisted to fend for themselves around those sputtering fires whipped by the stormy gales that tortured the top of this high, barren plateau. Howard's aide, First Lieutenant Melville C. Wilkinson, graciously named this spot "Camp Misery" in his daily report.

The following morning, 3 July, the advance command awoke to find that a dense fog had descended upon the mountaintop. While they remained in camp, recuperating and waiting for the pack train and infantry to catch up, the general dispatched Trimble's company and McConville's volunteers to search the trail ahead as far as they could march and still return by dusk. Late in the morning the patrol found the Nez Perce trail had split into two, the troopers following one branch, the civilians following the other. By late in the afternoon Trimble's patrol bivouacked where those two fresh trails rejoined—a place where Canoe Encampment and Rocky Canyon trails intersected. From all the sign, it appeared the last Nez Perce camp was at least three days old.

This meant that here late on the afternoon of 3 July Howard's column was now something on the order of four or more days behind the hostiles.

With little food and not a swallow of coffee to speak of—but with all the rain, fog, and wind an Irishman from Nova Scotia could ever hope for—on top of everything else now they knew just how far ahead the enemy was. McCarthy was afeared the hostiles never would stop and give an accounting of themselves—so he could get in his licks for all those comrades who had fallen at White Bird.

Blessed Mary and Joseph! Oh, how Sergeant Michael McCarthy prayed those goddamned heathens would stop running away and give this army a fight to decide the matter, once and for all.

"CAPTAIN WHIPPLE!" LIEUTENANT Sevier M. Rains called out as he stepped up to his company commander. "I brought those two civilians you asked for."

Whipple turned on his stool, positioned behind his field desk standing just outside his tent, and gave his second lieutenant a salute that early chill morning. "Very good, Mr. Rains. Please stay. I want you in on this."

Rains nodded. "Very good, sir." He pointed to the closest of the two Mount Idaho volunteers. "This is Foster, and this is Blewett."

"Your nominal leader, Captain D. B. Randall, said I could depend on you to get me some intelligence."

"Intelligence, Captain?" William Foster repeated.

"We need to know what we're facing here," Whipple explained. "What bands are in the area. If there are war parties prowling the nearby Camas Prairie. That sort of thing. Captain Randall claimed you two know this area better than the others."

"We know it," Charles Blewett affirmed. "Been on this prairie a few years. So we know the ground, and we know the Injuns, too. Never would've figgered Looking Glass's people for turning bad on us the way they did up on Clear Creek."

"I want you volunteers to find out what's become of those Indians," Whipple said. "They've had plenty of time to make it onto the prairie since yesterday morning. With Colonel Perry's supply train due along here from Fort Lapwai any day now, I don't want any war parties slipping up and surprising us."

"Better to know what the bastards are up to and where they're going," Blewett agreed.

Foster asked, "You gonna send some soldiers along with us, Captain?"

"No, more men would just make you a bigger target, easier to spot. With just the two of you, I figure any roving war parties won't spot you so easy." Then, in afterthought, Whipple added, "I don't figure you'll be all that far from this road station that you can't make a fast dash back here if you confront any ticklish situation."

"Awright, Captain," Foster replied. "We'll get us some rations and ride out."

Whipple nodded. "Can you make it over to the country by Craig's Landing, see if the hostiles are on the river, and get back by supper to make your report?"

"Back before dark," Blewett assured.

Whipple had established his camp a day ago among the deserted, ransacked buildings then known as the Norton ranch. The captain had brought his battalion here early yesterday, 2 July, after returning to Mount Idaho at midnight on the first, the day his command had destroyed Looking Glass's village. Captain Lawrence S. Babbitt, a member of General O. O. Howard's staff, was waiting for them there with written orders for Whipple to establish this presence at the Cottonwood road station. There he was to await Perry and his supply train, as well as intercepting, if possible, the Nez Perce if they should happen along his way after recrossing the Salmon.

"The general commanding orders that if Perry does not arrive with his supply train in a timely manner," Whipple had told his handful of battalion officers before they put Mount Idaho behind them yesterday, "I am to leave no stone unturned to ascertain where the Indians are heading. We are to report to the general by courier as often as we can." Then, the captain read another sentence from the note brought by Babbitt: " 'I expect of the cavalry tremendous vigor and activity even if it should kill a few horses.' "

Have no doubt about it: Howard wanted Joseph caught, corralled, and defeated.

When they had put Mount Idaho behind them yesterday, Lieutenant Rains wasn't sure how any of them should feel about that. This small battalion augmented by a few undisciplined civilians wasn't meant to confront and give battle to the hostile Nez Perce who had demolished Perry's command at the White Bird. Laying into Looking Glass's small village was one thing, but ordered to stand in the middle of this open prairie and bar the way of that band of heathen cutthroats, murderers, and rapists was altogether different. If Howard figured the hostiles were coming this way, then why the hell wasn't he here with reinforcements?

So Rains wholeheartedly agreed with the tactical decision Captain Whipple made regarding gathering intelligence on the wandering, dispossessed people of Looking Glass. Better to know what your enemy was doing than for any-thing to hit you as a total surprise. In the meantime, Colonel Perry would be coming down from Lapwai with supplies and ammunition, and maybe the advance of Howard's cavalry would make it in, too. In another day or so there would be enough soldiers here to put an end to the great Nez Perce war with a dying whimper.

Norton's road ranch was the only structural complex of any consequence on the whole of the Camas Prairie. Originally laid out in a wide brush- and tree-lined gulch along the south side of Cottonwood Creek some twenty miles west of its junction with the Clearwater, the house, barns, stables, and corrals overlapped the Mount Idaho–Lewiston Road. The house itself, where Jennie Norton had run her hotel business, sat on the south side of the creek.

Fifteen years before, a settler named Allen had built the original way sta-tion, consisting of a store, a saloon, a few hotel rooms, and a stage stop. The next year it sold to a pair of enterprising men, but within a year they had sold it to another man. John Byrom operated the place until Joseph Moore and Peter H. Ready of Mount Idaho bought the station. When they sold it to Ben-jamin and Jennie Norton, Moore stayed on to work for the new owners and Ready started hauling freight up and down the road to Lewiston,* which ran northwest from the ranch through a rolling countryside broken by some deep ravines carved by the tiny streams and rivulets feeding Cottonwood Creek.

Hearing stories told at Mount Idaho about the war party's raid conducted against the civilians and Ben Norton's death back on 14 June, when the Nez Perce outbreak was just getting under way, Rains was completely surprised to discover that the hostiles hadn't put a torch to any of the buildings. Upon the battalion's arrival here at this peaceful place, the lieutenant had taken a deep breath of air and looked about, finding it hard to believe there was an Indian war breaking out—and that it had started here.

"You two going to search from along the hillside?" he asked as he came to a stop near the two civilians and their horses. Foster was rising to the saddle.

Blewett swept his arm across the slope of nearby Craig's Mountain. "It makes sense to. There's plenty of timber for cover while we have us a look over the other side to see them Injuns come over the Craig Billy Crossing."

Foster reined his horse in a half-circle and tapped it with his heels as both civilians started away. He said, "Yonder side of that ridge, Lieutenant . . . that be where we figger we'll find us some Injuns."

"JESUS GOD!" WILLIAM Foster hissed under his breath as he yanked back on the horse's reins, his heart suddenly a lump in his throat.

Beside him, Charles Blewett spotted the large herd of horses at the same moment. Together their animals dug in their hooves and slid to a stop on the bare slope.

That herd of Indian ponies had suddenly appeared around the brow of a

---

*Cries from the Earth, vol. 14, the Plainsmen series.

nearby hill barren of timber, north of the Cottonwood near the road to Fort Lapwai and Lewiston.

"That ain't no loose stock," Blewett said as they both quickly glanced this way and that for possible cover.

"They'll have herders with 'em," Foster grumbled the moment before he spotted the riders arrayed on the flanks of the large herd.

At this distance, he could tell those outriders wore feathers and carried weapons. No youngsters these. A war party for damned sure.

Foster started to wheel his pony around, saying, "Let's get afore they—"

But he was interrupted by the first pop of a far-off rifle.

As the sun had come out and their damp clothing began to steam that morning following days of hard, intermittent rain, the two civilians had traveled northwest on the Lewiston stage road to the point where it crossed Boardhouse Creek, then angled off to the left on the Salmon River Trail in the direction of Lawyer's Canyon. It had been a trail that took them over a long, rolling ridge before it descended into a little open saddle, then climbed once more up the shallow slope at the southwest side of Craig's Mountain.

That's where the broad, open terrain butted up against some light timber on this east side of the mountain rising more than a thousand feet above the Cottonwood. They were two ridges away from the soldier camp when they spotted the herd . . . and those warriors.

Jerking his head around to look over his shoulder at the distant gunshot, Foster saw the puff of smoke drifting on the cool wind, finding more than a handful of the warriors already galloping full-tilt in their direction.

"You don't need to ask me to get more'n once!" Blewett screamed as he flailed the side of his horse with the long reins.

Foster pointed as his horse shot him past Blewett's. "We make that brush, maybe we can lose 'em!"

The pair of civilians had covered no more than a hundred yards when Foster heard his friend call out with the sort of cry that instantly brought a chill to a man's spine.

"Bill!"

It took a moment for Foster to yank back on the reins and get his hell-bent-for-leather horse to slow to a halt. By the time he could turn the animal around in place, he watched Blewett finish his brief flight through the air, hitting the ground, hard, on his hip—his horse rearing back on its hind legs and pawing the air before it came down on all fours and tore off, riderless.

"Goddammit, Bill!"

"I'll go catch that damned horse for you!"

Before he got very far, Foster heard the first snarl of a bullet passing by his head, watching first one, then another, of the Indian guns spew gunsmoke in the distance as the half-dozen warriors approached at a gallop. That's when he realized he wasn't going to reach Blewett's horse in time to pick him up and ride on out of there with his friend. The horse was tearing off hell-for-leather toward Lawyer's Canyon, too damned close to those warriors.

"Get hid!" Foster screamed loud as he could while he sawed back the reins, shoving down on the stirrups, wrenching his horse around in mid-stride. "I'm goin' for help."

"*No!*" Blewett pleaded in dismay from the distance, hands up and imploring. "Come back an' get me yourself! We kin ride double—"

"I'll bring some soldiers!" Foster promised. "Get hid in the brush, Charlie! Get hid!"

Then he was pummelling the horse's ribs again, no longer able to look at that frightened, pasty blur of Blewett's face. The dismay, the terror, written there as he had to hear the pounding hooves straining ever closer.

William Foster had just made his best friend a promise. And a man never broke a promise to a friend.

He'd get some of the captain's soldiers and they'd hurry back to drive off the small war party. It wouldn't take long for him to reach Cottonwood Station from here, Foster told himself as another bullet whined past his ear. It wouldn't take him long to bring back some help.

After all, William Foster never broke his promise.

CHAPTER FOURTEEN

---◆---

Khoy-Tsahl, 1877

EE HOW THE TWO OF THEM RUN!" SHORE CROSSING ROARED TO HIS cousin as the two riders in the distance wheeled and bolted away.

Red Moccasin Tops, the one called *Sarpsis Ilppilp* by their people, laughed. "I haven't seen men run so afraid since we chased the *suapies* and their Shadow friends from the valley of *Lahmotta!*"

Already Rainbow and Five Wounds, another pair of inseparable warrior friends, were yelping, too, waving their rifles as their ponies shot away from the herd they were guiding back to their camp on the upper Cottonwood. It was a bright and beautiful morning after many days of intermittent rain and wind. Nothing more than a light breeze had blown in their faces as they started some captured Shadow horses back for the village. The sun felt good on the bare skin stretched across Shore Crossing's tawny, sinewy limbs.

"Come ride after the Shadows with us, Swan Necklace!" Shore Crossing cried to his younger nephew.

"*Eeh!*" the one called *Wetyetmas Wahyakt* cried back in youthful glee. He wasn't nearly as old as his two companions, no more than twenty summers old now. "We haven't shot our guns at any Shadows since we fired them at Cut-Off Arm's soldiers when he started to cross the river *Tahmonah!*"

In a broad line the warriors were streaming away from the herd now, right behind Rainbow and Five Wounds, the two daring warriors who had rejoined the bands the very day of the fight that had brought a resounding defeat for the soldiers. Two Moons, called *Lepeet Hessemdooks*, rode on the far right flank. And the strong and powerful *Otskai*, known as Going Out, brought up the left.

Shore Crossing, this young man called *Wahlitits*, had been the catalyst of this war. What had started out as his hunger to prove himself a man before a pretty young woman in those days of *Hillal* at their traditional gathering ground of *Tepahlewam*, had soon blown itself into a general uprising. So much the better! For now all the People had fallen in behind Shore Crossing's daring act to finally avenge the wrongful death of his father many winters ago.

Eagle Robe, known as *Tipyalhlanah Siskon*, had consented to loan a conniving Shadow named Larry Ott some of his land to graze a few cattle and horses while the *Nee-Me-Poo* rode east into the buffalo country. But when White Bird's band returned and Eagle Robe went to ask the Shadow to leave his land near the mouth of Deer Creek, Ott had pulled his gun and shot Shore Crossing's father.

When Eagle Robe did not return for the longest time, *Wahlitits* went looking for him, only to find his father dying against Larry Ott's fence.

"Please," Eagle Robe begged. "Promise me . . . promise me you will not take vengeance—"

"I cannot!" his son had shrieked.

For the longest time Eagle Robe had tried to speak, but no sound came from his tongue; none crossed his bloodied lips. He was about to die . . . and Shore Crossing knew he could not let his father die without hearing the words he so wanted to hear his son speak.

Eventually, Shore Crossing spoke softly, very reluctantly, and most sadly.

"I promise you, Father."

Eagle Robe had closed his eyes at last. *Wahlitits* heard that last breath gush up in a ball from his father's punctured lungs as his head gently sagged to the side.

Anguished, Shore Crossing had sobbed, pressing his head against his father's bloody breast, "I promise . . . promise not to kill this man who has killed you!"

But . . . that had been back when he considered himself a boy.

In the last three winters since his father's murder, *Wahlitits* had grown to manhood and taken a wife. Just this last spring she had announced she was carrying their first child.

"Maybe you want another woman because your first wife is growing bigger, eh?" Red Moccasin Tops had asked him that first day of their search for Larry Ott. Shore Crossing had been making soft eyes at a young woman in Joseph's band.

Bringing Swan Necklace along as their horse holder, the trio hadn't found the murderer, so they went in search of another man who had mistreated the *Nee-Me-Poo* before, even setting his dogs on them. After Richard Divine was killed, they remembered Jurden Elfers had many fine horses and were sure that he had some guns, too. They shot the horse breeder and three[*] more men before starting back for *Tepahlewam* to the village—where the whole camp came alive with war fever. Sun Necklace,[**] the father of Red Moccasin Tops, led out the first band of warriors who were hot to spill some more blood of the Salmon River settlers who had done them so much wrong for many seasons.

Now they had defeated the *suapies* in the canyon of *Lahmotta*, then led Cut-Off Arm's soldiers on a merry chase through the Salmon River breaks while the village had recrossed to camp at *Aipadass*, a sagebrush flat just north of Craig Billy Crossing, where the village had rested for a day before starting across the Camas Prairie for the Clearwater this morning.

---

[*]Shore Crossing and Red Moccasin Tops killed only four of five men they shot in their first spasm of revenge; Samuel Benedict was only wounded and feigned death until the war starters rode away.

[**]This is the historical figure who, after the Nez Perce War, changed his name to Yellow Bull (*Chuslum Moxmox*)—as recorded by most of the war's historians.

Whooping and shrieking in glee this warm summer day, the exuberant warriors sped after the two fleeing Shadows. Like those raids of burning, raping, and murder, this chase, too, was nothing less than great fun. Too bad there were only two of the Boston men—a term the *Nee-Me-Poo* had long, long used to indicate the pale-skinned traders who had come among them bringing goods from afar, carried on ships that plied the far oceans.

Wahlitits and *Sarpsis Ilppilp* had grown up together, more like brothers than cousins. Much more than cousins, they were best friends in everything. Red Moccasin Tops was an excitable young man, part Cayuse in blood, in fact a grandson of *Tomahas*, one of the murderers of missionaries Marcus and Narcissa Whitman many years before.

"He's mine!" Rainbow shouted the moment the Shadow was pitched off his rearing horse less than two hundred yards away.

"No!" protested Five Wounds, Rainbow's best friend since childhood. "It was my shot made him fall!"

"You two argue all you want over the one who is put on foot!" Strong Eagle bellowed. This capable warrior called *Tipyahlahnah Kapskaps*, like Shore Crossing and Red Moccasin Tops, had tied a red blanket at his neck as they rode into battle against the *suapies* at the White Bird. From that morning the three were known as the "Red Coats."

Strong Eagle brought his rifle to his shoulder, preparing to fire. "I want the other Shadow who thinks he is getting away!"

"You will not be so lucky today, Strong Eagle!" screamed Shore Crossing. "That foolish Shadow is mine!"

The other Red Coat snorted with a wide grin, "Only if that poor horse of yours is faster than mine!"

"Farewell, *Wahlitits!*" cried Red Moccasin Tops as he pulled his pony aside for the Shadow put afoot. "I am going after the one hiding in the brush like a scared rabbit!"

"There is no sport in that!" Shore Crossing chided his cousin. "No bravery running down some poor, frightened ground squirrel who has soiled himself in fear of us!"

They laughed as they parted company, some of them streaming right after the Shadow scampering into the timber and brush on foot, while the others galloped after the fleeing rider. *Wahlitits*, Strong Eagle, Five Wounds, and Rainbow were closing the gap on the big horse that had grown weary of the long run. Shadow horses may look pretty, but they simply did not have the mighty lungs the *Nee-Me-Poo* bred into their ponies. And that dramatic difference was showing as they dashed up this long, gradual slope, tearing through the green grass growing tall here in midsummer radiance. The Shadow disappeared momentarily over the top of the grassy knoll.

"Now we will catch him!" Shore Crossing shouted as he brought the long rawhide strands of his quirt down against his pony's rear flanks. "It will be a race between him and me to the Cottonwood!"

The last word was barely off his tongue when the four of them reached the top of that bare hill and started down the long slope after the Shadow— gazing far beyond the single rider to that gulch where stood all the buildings of the white family . . . suddenly finding more *suapies* encamped there than Shore Crossing could count. Tiny, dark figures only—but, there must be at least ten-times-ten of them!

Where had they come from?

"Ho! Ho!" Rainbow called, throwing up his hand as he yanked back on the horsehair rein wrapped around his horse's lower jaw.

Why were these soldiers camped here on the upper reaches of the Cottonwood? Did they intend to attack the Non-Treaty camp? Perhaps they were planning to march all the way down the creek so they could prevent the warrior bands from forming a junction with Looking Glass's people on the Clearwater?

"Let him go, *Wahlitits!*" Five Wounds ordered gruffly.

Shore Crossing was the last to stop his horse, finally halting farther down the slope than the others. His pony was lathered and excited, having just caught its second wind, raring to finish the race its rider had started it on. The animal pranced round and round, tossing its head in protest.

"I know; I know," he told it, bringing the horse under control, patting its damp neck. "Angry disappointment sours in my stomach, too. I could almost feel that Shadow's hot blood on my hands!"

"RIDER COMING!"

Second Lieutenant Sevier M. Rains turned at that strident cry from one of the outlying pickets. In fact, there wasn't a man in Whipple's battalion who didn't immediately stop what he was doing and turn to watch that lone civilian streaking down the long slope toward the wide gulch where their bivouac stood among the abandoned buildings of Cottonwood Station.

Just as he was shading his eyes with a hand, Rains watched at least four horsemen break the skyline right behind the lone rider. From the looks of things, they had been gaining on the civilian and—had not the soldiers' bivouac been where it was—those Nez Perce warriors would have clearly turned the scout into a victim.

"Where's the other'n, sir?" asked Private Franklin Moody.

Private David Carroll replied before the rest, "I s'pose he ain't coming back at all."

"We don't know that!" Whipple snapped as he lumbered out of his tent, yanking on his blue blouse with its two rows of small brass buttons sewn down the front. He stopped at Rains's elbow.

"Captain, he can't be bringing us good news," the young lieutenant said quietly, hoping that most of the enlisted would not hear.

For a long moment, Whipple gazed at his second lieutenant. Then he said, "Mr. Rains, you're my most trusted second. As adjutant of this command, I want you to select five men from our L Company, and call out five more from Captain Winters's E."

"Rescue detail, sir?"

"Exactly," Whipple answered, roughly shoving the last button through its hole, every man around him watching one warrior slowly turn his horse around and rejoin the others at the brow of the hill, where they eventually disappeared from view. "You'll go in the advance and I will come on your rear with a larger force in your support. A word of caution: don't extend yourself too far, keep on the high ground, and report back to my command at the first sign of the Indians."

"Fifty rounds for our carbines?" Rains asked.

"Yes—and your service revolvers will require another twenty-four."

Rains wheeled on Moody, excitement hot in his veins. "Private, now you and Carroll have the chance to ride with me."

"Sir, respectin' your authority an' all," Moody replied, "but them red bastards is just gonna run when they see us riding out after 'em."

Rains's eyes crinkled with a smile as he replied, "Then we'll all just get a chance to see a little more of the country as we chase the buggers off. Now you and Carroll go draw three hundred rounds of carbine ammo and one hundred and fifty cartridges for our Colts. I'm going to call out the rest of the detail."

Captain Henry E. Winters was returning from the trench latrine dug in a dry wash downwind of camp, his shirttails flying as Rains met him in the middle of the company street. The lieutenant quickly explained Whipple's orders, at which Winters began calling out the first five men of E Company he spotted nearby. From nothing more than their names, the young lieutenant immediately figured they all had to be Irishmen. Seven Irishmen in all now, along with his three Germans.

It was Foster who galloped into camp gripping that half-crazed, snorting horse on the verge of lathering. The civilian was swinging out of the saddle and lunging to the ground even before the animal had completed its bouncing, four-legged skid to a halt.

"Captain Whipple!" he gasped as more than half a hundred soldiers pressed close to listen.

"You are?"

"William F-Foster." He breathed it hard. Not so much from any exertion as from the hot flush of adrenaline that must be shooting through his veins.

"Where's the other one? I sent two of you out. What happened to—"

"His horse bucked him off," Foster interrupted. "Too far back for me to get him, too close to the Injuns for me to pull 'im up to ride double with me—"

"You left the man?" Rains interrupted now accusingly, taking a step right up to the civilian's knee.

Foster glared at the lieutenant, jaw jutting. "I'll take you back, any of you man enough to go," he rasped. "Get me a fresh horse and we'll go back for Blewett."

Whipple put his hand on Rains's shoulder. "The lieutenant here is preparing to do just that, Mr. Foster. Sergeant! Get this civilian a fresh horse, immediately!"

In less than ten minutes the lieutenant's detail was armed and mounted, moving out as a trumpeter played "Boots and Saddles" in that bivouac they put at their backs. Rains and his men followed William Foster, who had climbed atop a fresh army horse. The civilian rocked forward, then backward, trying to get comfortable in the McClellan saddle already cinched around the belly of the animal given him to ride.

"Wish I'd swapped for my own saddle, Lieutenant."

"Don't you fret, Mr. Foster." Rains kept his eyes on the brow of that hill where the half-naked horsemen had disappeared as soon as they spotted the soldier camp. "I don't believe we'll be in the saddle all that long. Just enough time to collect your friend, perhaps learn what we can as to the location of that war party jumped you, then return to our camp."

"Location?" Foster repeated. "You mean you're going to follow them warriors to find out where the sonsabitches are camped?"

"No," Rains replied, tugging at that leather glove he wore on his left hand, the one he had pulled over his West Point class ring. "But if we happen to see the direction they ride off in . . . that will be a good indication of where their village lies. All the better for us to protect that pack train due down from Fort Lapwai any time now."

CHAPTER FIFTEEN

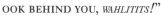

Khoy-Tsahl, 1877

Cottonwood, 4 P.M. (Tuesday)

*One of our scouts just in reports seeing twelve or more Indians
from here toward Salmon River. On returning he was fired upon
by a single Indian and he and the other scout returned the shots.
In some way one scout was dismounted and took to the brush and
the other was obliged to leave him. These Indians were coming
from the direction of the Salmon river on the trail leading toward
Kamai and crossing the road passing the place about eight miles
from here. The whole command starts in a few moments and may
bag the outfit unless the whole of Joseph's force is present.*

Babbitt, commanding.

LOOK BEHIND YOU, *WAHLITITS!*"

He twisted half-way around on the bare back of his pony when
Red Moccasin Tops shouted and pointed. A long way back, they
were coming. A short, wriggling worm of *suapies* riding out from
that soldier camp down in the Cottonwood gulch. Already, *Seeyakoon Ilppilp*,
the young warrior called Red Spy, had killed the lone Shadow who had taken
refuge in the brush, and came riding back to show off the dead man's guns.

"Five Wounds! We must find a place where we can greet these Shadows!" *Wahlitits* cried in anticipation. Shore Crossing could feel the excitement flushing away the disappointment that had surged through him when
he had to give up the chase minutes ago.

"Yes!" Five Wounds cried with similar enthusiasm. "Up there in those
trees. We'll wait for the others. Red Moccasin Tops—go get them. Tell Two
Moons we have some good quarry coming and we want them to help us
close the trap."

Shore Crossing asked, "We'll put the Shadows between us?"

This time Rainbow smiled. "Yes. We'll wait to ride out of the timber until
they are past us."

"Then they will be caught between you and Two Moons's men!" Red
Moccasin Tops whooped, taking off like a shot, shrieking in glee.

It was a long time to wait, those heartbeats while they kept an eye pinned on the approaching Shadows. At times none of the warriors could see the soldiers for the broken hillsides, then the short line of *suapies* would reappear from behind a slope, still coming on and on. As they got closer and closer, finally passing just below the copse of dark timber where the warriors waited in the shadows, Shore Crossing could see how the white men kept turning their heads this way and that. Not only did they appear to be keeping their eyes open for an ambush, but they seemed to be looking down for something in the tall grass—

Then *Wahlitits* remembered. "The other rider!" he whispered to Five Wounds beside him. "They're searching the grass, looking for the other dead man!"

Close enough, they could hear the persistent cough of one of the soldiers who slowly passed by them just down the slope. He was not a well man—his cough sounding full of noisy water. Then the *suapies* had moved on by. And Shore Crossing found himself all but squirming on the back of his pony, anxious to get about the killing.

Rainbow inched his pony forward one length, then turned it so he could face the others. "When we ride out of the trees, we must race down the slope *behind* the soldiers. That way we will keep them up the hill from us."

"And that way the Shadows can't get out of our trap by racing downhill," Shore Crossing said, anticipation squirting through his veins. "We must go now! Hurry before the others kill them all!"

"These are not unarmed Shadows asleep in their beds, *Wahlitits*," Rainbow scolded. "These are soldiers."

"I fought soldiers at *Lahmotta!*" Shore Crossing snapped angrily, wounded by the criticism. "I wore my red coat for the enemy to see me! And I rode right past their lines, time after time!"

"Which is why we don't want any of these soldiers to escape us today the way some soldiers escaped from *Lahmotta*," Five Wounds emphasized. "Let them get a little farther on the hillside before we ride down on them. There—you see that low brush on the slope ahead of them?"

"Yes," Rainbow answered. "Near those low rocks?"

"Yes—we will have Strong Eagle stay in sight by that dead pine tree while we turn back to the timber uphill. *Tipyahlahnah Kapskaps* will be the decoy to bring those soldiers on and on," Five Wounds explained his plan. "When they have gone past those rocks, the rest of us will ride out and show ourselves, then chase them into the ground."

"LIEUTE*NANT!*"

Rains heard the war whoops and those hoofbeats at the same moment the rest of them realized the Nez Perce were swooping up behind them.

"They want to get between us and our relief!" the lieutenant shouted. "Shut off our escape! But they don't realize Captain Whipple is coming!"

"There ain't that many of 'em," Private William Roche said.

Private Patrick Quinn agreed. "We can knock 'em all down, Lieutenant!"

Yanking back on his reins, Rains spun his horse around in a half-circle, staring farther up the slope at the barren hilltop. In an instant he realized he had been a little too eager, too anxious to distinguish himself—and had outrun his support. In too much of a hurry the lieutenant had followed Foster along the ridge that angled away from the valley of the Cottonwood toward Craig's Mountain. After loping two quick miles to the northwest of Norton's ranch, the scout led them down into a broad swale before they began their gentle ascent of the mountain slope. At their rear now, cutting south from the saddle, extended a shallow coulee, but . . . Whipple and his support were nowhere in sight.

"We better get onto the high ground, men," Rains ordered the instant he caught sight of those warriors. He knew they could hold out until Whipple's outfit arrived in a matter of minutes. "C'mon!"

They had just kicked their horses into motion, these dozen men no longer clustered in formation—no more than thirty yards from the top of that rise when the patch of skyline that had been their destination suddenly bristled with at least eighteen warriors.

"Shit!" Private John Burk cried as they all sawed backward on their reins, horses colliding with one another, bumping their riders as they milled and wheeled about.

"I'll take my chances against them others behind us!" Sergeant Charles Lampman roared. "Ain't as many!"

"We can ride right through 'em!" Private Daniel Ryan proposed, pointing.

Private Frederick Meyer bobbed his head. "Ride through 'em. We can do that, can't we, Lieutenant?"

His eyes scanned the distance, quickly trying to calculate how far back it would be to make their run, to figure just how long before Whipple would show up on the next hilltop. Foster had done it. The civilian had made it back in one piece. Maybe they could ride downhill right through that smaller band of warriors and be at a full gallop before the rest could be on their tails—

"Them rocks, Lieutenant!" Lampman shouted, pointing along the slope. "We can hold out in them rocks!"*

At that moment those boulders seemed to be a far smarter idea. Far more inviting than a long, ten-mile horse race back to Cottonwood. Rains hollered, "To the rocks!"

Private Otto H. Richter was the first to start at an angle for the boulders, William Roche right behind him. Rains twisted around in the saddle as the others broke past him. "C'mon, Dinteman! Ride, goddammit, man!"

The private was having trouble with his mount. The animal side-stepped as George H. Dinteman kicked and flailed it, trying to goad it into motion. Just as it started to rear onto its hind legs, the horse suddenly twisted aright and flung itself into motion. The private was suddenly ahead of him, less than a full length . . . making them the last two riding for the rocks—

That sound was like no other on earth. He immediately remembered what his father—that great Confederate hero—had repeatedly said: A man always heard the bullet that got him.

---

*These rocks, still visible today on private property, are actually some 750 feet south of the old Lewiston–Mount Idaho Road.

But by the time Second Lieutenant Sevier M. Rains turtled his head into his shoulders, the bullet had already passed and struck the private in the back less than three yards ahead of him. Dinteman screwed off his horse, his arms flailing, hung momentarily in the off-hand stirrup, then was flung free to tumble through the grass like a sock doll.

Rains shot past the private before he could react, yanking back and sawing the reins to the side at the same time. For a moment he could not locate Dinteman in the tall grass; then he saw the private's knee sticking up. Just the one knee. Unmoving. And coming on at a full gallop was not just one bunch of bare-chested, feathered, screeching horsemen but a second: streaming out of the broad coulee behind them!

Dinteman was dead already. If he still breathed, Rains told himself, it wouldn't be for long. Since he wasn't moving, then he couldn't help in his own rescue—and the lieutenant realized he didn't have enough time to make that rescue on his own. Step out of the saddle, kneel and lift the deadweight, hurl it onto the back of his horse, then remount . . . none of that was possible now.

There went Foster, the son of a bitch, racing off to the south on his own. Rains hated him: a man who could run away from his friend minutes ago, and now the civilian was scampering away from this fight. The lieutenant almost felt good a moment later when he watched a bullet knock Foster off his horse and a pair of warriors ride up to fire down at the body sprawled in the tall grass—

"Lieutenant!"

One of Winters's men was shouting, standing exposed there in the smaller of the two rings of low boulders. Patrick Quinn, good Irishman that he was. The private was waving Rains in, urging him on.

As Rains wheeled his horse and goaded it with those small brass knobs at the back of his spurs, he gradually sensed something not quite right. Quinn's face suddenly began to swim, growing more and more watery as the horse carried him closer and closer to the boulders. The lieutenant looked down, saw the black molasses stain of blood spreading across his belly, seeping into his crotch.

"Hep! Hep!" he growled at the horse, angry at himself for getting shot, then yanked at the bottom of his blue blouse, pulling it up to have a close look at the wound.

A small finger of intestine was already protruding from the exit wound. As he watched, more of the gut squirted from that ragged hole with every rugged lunge of his exhausted horse. By the time Quinn and Moody grabbed hold of the bridle and were dragging him down out of the saddle, Rains had his forearm filled with his own sticky gut.

"Set me down! Set me down where I can shoot!" he shouted at them through gritted, bloody teeth. Bright crimson gushed up at the back of his throat, hot and thick. He struggled to swallow his gorge back down. Better that than to puke it up in front of his men.

Lord Almighty, Rains thought as they positioned him against the rocks and knelt around him, *a gut wound is a slow way to die. A damned slow way to die.*

"Make every shot count!" Quinn was reminding the others for him. "Shoot low for the horses first!"

Sergeant Lampman whined, "And ours run off with the ammo!"

"Hol' . . . hold 'em back till Whipple hears the gunfire. He can't be far now," Rains told his men, wanting to inspire more hope in them than he felt for himself.

Out there in the grass, the warriors were swarming over the first of the six wounded men who hadn't made it into these rocks, each of those soldiers shrieking in terror and pain, their high voices more shrill and grating than the war cries—

A Nez Perce bullet spun John Burk around. He landed across the lieutenant's legs. Ryan dragged the body off Rains, knelt again, and continued to fire with his carbine.

Rains continued to speak in a practiced, even tone. *Gotta keep their spirits up.* "We can do this. We can do this, men. One of you, give me Burk's carbine. Load it and put it in my hands."

Lampman had just handed Rains the dead man's carbine as more than ten of the warriors dismounted and spread out in a broad front to fire their weapons when Lampman himself was hit, low in the back of his head. Blood and brain matter splattered over Rains's face as the private fell atop Burk, knocking the lieutenant's carbine aside.

With a great exertion of conscious thought, Rains picked the carbine up, his gloves gummy with blood. So much blood.

Just how in Hades did you go through the whole of two goddamned wars and never get a scratch, Father dear?

A brigadier goddamned general—that's how, he thought as he brought the sticky carbine to his cheek and gazed down the barrel at the warriors popping up out there in the grass.

Someone groaned and fell into the grass out there to his right. Dying noisily. Rains prayed the man would die quick. Sounded like Roche. *Godblesshim.*

How did my own father command a guard of soldiers that protected the Walla Walla councils back in 1855, out here in this northwest territory, and not suffer one damned wound? How had my father played a role in the multitribal wars that followed those councils . . . and not once have a bullet blow a hole through his belly?

"Goddamned lucky, weren't you?"

"What did you say, Lieutenant?" Quinn asked.

"Nothing," Rains said, his tongue thick with blood. "Just . . . we've got to keep them from getting any closer in that grass. They can hide. So, shoot low up that hill, men. Shoot low and conserve your cartridges until Whipple gets here with relief."

Richter was next out there in the grass. Then Moody right behind him. The bullets that hit them shoved both soldiers back into the grass as they were crabbing toward the rocks. Not a good thing. The red bastards could see how few of them were still alive.

Ryan whimpered when a bullet slammed into the side of his head. But he didn't make noise for long. Almost immediately, Quinn was bending over his bunkie, laying the dying soldier down before he bent over to pick up his friend's carbine—when the private was hit twice and his own body flopped over Ryan in a leg-twitching sprawl.

The next time Rains threw back the trapdoor on his carbine, he found a cartridge already shoved into the breech. For a moment he thought the extractor wasn't working, that the empty cartridge had been fused into the chamber with heat and verdigris—but he was able to extract the copper case from the weapon, finding it hadn't been fired.

"You stupid son of a bitch," he cursed himself as he shoved the cartridge back into the action and snapped the trapdoor closed over it.

He had been so intent on watching the warriors crawl up through the grass, watching as those six men were picked off and whittled down one by one, that he had forgotten to fire the damned carbine after reloading it.

The forestock was gummier as he brought it up to his cheek, aimed at a figure in the grass, then pulled the trigger.

While he was reloading with his sticky, bloody gloves, pulling a shell from Ryan's pocket, he willed his eyes to make a count. All the rest were down.

Getting so weak, barely able to lift the weapon . . . by the time he could get the carbine back into position, Rains found David Carroll lying in a heap out there twenty yards away, curled up like a cat on an autumn day, groaning and pawing at the bubbling wound low in his chest.

Who in Hades is going to hold off the red bastards till Whipple arrives? Everyone else gone already. I'm the only one for them to save now.

For a moment he stared at two of them lying here, close enough for him to touch: Quinn had been driven backward by the impact of the bullet that had killed him, hurtled against the low rock where he had been kneeling, then slid down to crumple across Richter.

Irish and German, Rains thought as he stared at their death masks. *Only one of us for Whipple to save now. All the Irish and German dead. Wasn't for the Irish and German . . . there'd be no goddamned frontier army.*

Gradually he became aware of the quiet. So very, very quiet as he fumbled in Ryan's pocket for another cartridge. Empty. Maybe Burk there had some. Where was the man in this jumble of arms and legs and blood and brain . . . and his own gut?

Grown so quiet out there now that he could hear the red bastards whispering, even hear the rustle of the tall grass as they moved closer.

Carefully, slowly—a few heads rose in the grass, dark eyes staring at him.

More than a dozen of them—

His fingers located a cartridge in Burk's pocket. Frantically he shoved it into the action as the warriors started to slink toward him in a half-crouch. The copper case pasted to the blood-crusted fingers of his gloves.

Maybe Whipple will hear now . . . now that things have gone so damned quiet up here.

Snapping the trapdoor down, he dragged the hammer back but found he didn't have the strength to raise the carbine to his shoulder. Rains could only position the butt against his lower chest. The instant he fired he realized his shot went wild, but the warriors nonetheless flung themselves into the grass momentarily.

With an ear-numbing shriek, in unison they rose as one and rushed him in a blur.

He watched the first, then a second and third gun explode, each muzzle spewing fire from close range. He felt the dull racket in his head; an instant later his chest was on fire.

Too late to call for Whipple. Too late.

But it was time to call for his father. *A brigadier goddamned general would know what to do now. Just call for the general.*

"Father . . . General . . . tell me, what am I to do now, s-sir? Help me. . . . Sh-show me now how a good officer dies."

CHAPTER SIXTEEN

———— ❖ ————

Khoy-Tsahl, 1877

THIS WAS BUT HIS TWENTY-FIRST SUMMER, BUT HE HAD HIMSELF KILLED four of the *suapies* who had come to attack their *Lahmotta* camp. Young though he might be, Yellow Wolf stood second in warrior rank only to *Ollokot,* Joseph's young brother.

Yellow Wolf had been the one who made the most noise out there in the grass below the boulders, jumping up to show himself here, then there. Never the same place twice as the others crept in, slowly, silently. This young warrior called *He-mene Mox Mox* made the noise in the grass, shouting and calling out to draw the horse soldiers' attention as Five Wounds led the others in for the kill.

Six of the *suapies* had fallen from their horses before the fight even began, hit during the last mad scramble. The other half barely made it to those low rocks before Yellow Wolf's friends got started on the serious killing. When the rest made the last rush, there was but one last shot fired from the white man. As their bullets struck that last Shadow, his rifle slowly spilled from his hands covered with those bloody gloves.

Yellow Wolf knelt before him, looking into the man's face, seeing how it was drenched with blood from that bullet hole almost directly between the soldier's eyes. Blinking repeatedly, the white man seemed to stare right through Yellow Wolf, his lips starting to move, sticky with the blood that drenched the Shadow. Yet all that came out of the soldier's mouth was a chicken sound . . . *cluck. Cluck. Cluck. Cluck—*

"Do you know what he is saying in the Shadow tongue?" asked Five Wounds as the older warrior knelt beside the inquisitive Yellow Wolf.

"No. I never learned any of the white man talk," Yellow Wolf replied. Then he looked deep into the man's eyes, saw the eyelashes coated thickly with blood that seeped from that bullet wound between the eyes. Noticed the way the soldier looked right on through him as if he weren't there. "Maybe," he said to Five Wounds and the others who were starting to pilfer through the pockets of the other five soldiers, "this one is asking me to help him die quicker."

"Perhaps that's true, that he cannot live," *Wahlitits* said. "His body is too badly hurt."

Red Moccasin Tops added, "But he still lives. He is a strong warrior, refusing to die. He is like *Nee-Me-Poo.*"

Five Wounds shook his head. "No Shadow is like us. But, this one is strong enough to live if he wants to. But he has to want to live."

Old *Dookiyoon*, known as Smoker, took his ancient flintlock horse pistol from his belt and wagged the muzzle near the soldier's left ear. That gun had belonged to his family for three generations—handed down from the early days of contact with the Boston Men.

"We cannot leave him like this," Smoker said with a hint of sadness to his voice. "He will be too long in dying."

"And he was a brave fighter," Yellow Wolf asserted with a measure of respect. "He deserves to die quickly, this brave fighter."

Suddenly Smoker said, "Yes. Die quickly, brave fighter." And he immediately shoved the muzzle of his old pistol against the Shadow's chest, pulling the trigger.

The force of the big lead ball caused the white man to topple to the side, where he lay quietly, no longer clucking like a chicken scratching feed on the ground between lodges.

Yellow Wolf was just beginning to feel better about it when the body stirred and the soldier slowly, painfully, raised himself back to a sitting position there against the rocks splattered with some of the man's brain. Once the Shadow was upright, he began to quietly cluck again: his lips moving ever so slightly, the tip of his blood-thickened tongue appearing as he made his strange talking sound. Yellow Wolf wished he knew the white man's language. Then the eyes rolled slowly around, as if looking over the half-dozen or so warriors gathered closest to him. Those eyes studied Yellow Wolf's friends as blood continued to ooze from the head wound, dripping over the eyelids and lashes.

"Ho, ho, Smoker!" Red Moccasin Tops snorted with laughter. "Your old gun—it is weak as a young foal's penis! It did not kill this strong, strong Boston Man, even up close!"

Just as Smoker was about to argue, wrenching up his pouch to begin reloading the old flintlock pistol, Two Moons stepped up, clutching his *kopluts* in his hand. Without a word, he swung it against the side of the soldier's head with a hard crack that knocked the dying man over again.

"Stop!" Yellow Wolf yelled, waving his arms at the old warrior. "Get back, Two Moons! Get back from him!"

Five Wounds grabbed the young warrior by the elbow. "Yellow Wolf—it is all right what Two Moons does. He is doing what is best for this soldier now."

For a moment, Yellow Wolf looked at Two Moons's face, then reluctantly nodded as he looked down at the soldier, watching how the man struggled to breathe. "Yes. I see. We have no healer with us. Poor, poor Shadow—he is suffering." Then he drew in a long sigh. "All right. Maybe we should put him out of his trouble now."

"You, Yellow Wolf?" asked Two Moons.

"Yes."

The old man handed the young warrior his short-handled war club. Yellow Wolf gripped it securely, raised it over his shoulder, then drove it down into the top of the white man's head. The *suapie* grunted. Then he hit the soldier a second time. And the enemy made no more sound.

Bending on his knee, Yellow Wolf put his face down close to the soldier's, looking into those unblinking eyes, watching those bloody lips and tongue for any movement. There was none. And now he closed the eyes. They were no longer staring up at him, gazing into Yellow Wolf's soul and asking for assistance.

"You have helped him?" Five Wounds asked.

Rocking back on his haunches, Yellow Wolf handed the *kopluts* back to Two Moons. "Yes. The last one is dead now."

"CAN YOU BELIEVE that?" asked Captain Henry Winters. "They're pulling off!"

Stephen G. Whipple nodded in disbelief. "Even though they outnumber us, we've driven them off."

Minutes ago as he had listened to the faint, distant booming of the Springfield carbines, Whipple had been advancing with more than seventy of his enlisted, leaving their Cottonwood camp in the care of fewer than thirty soldiers and volunteers. Instead of riding to the sound of those guns, Whipple grew confused by the echo of that gunfire—halting his command on the eastern side of that low saddle while he studied the slope and timber above him.

Wondering why Rains had ridden out of sight. With that gunfire so near, Whipple surely expected to see the lieutenant and his detail come galloping right over the top of that ridge any moment now. He waited, waited . . . then the gunfire died off—

When suddenly a broad band of warriors arrayed themselves before his men at the top of the hill.

"Rains must have driven them off!" Whipple cheered to Winters. "He's driven them into us!"

Whipple dismounted the entire body and ordered horse holders to the rear, instantly reducing his tactical force by one-fourth. The rest he spread out on a wide front, double distances between each of the soldiers as more warriors appeared on the hillside, making bold and provocative movements along his skirmishers' front. Now there were more than a hundred of the enemy facing them, horsemen who occasionally fired their rifles and shouted at the soldiers.

It became painfully clear to the captain that Lieutenant Rains and his ten-man detail were not going to reappear, full of life, herding a small war party toward Whipple's seventy-man battalion. They were lost, swallowed up by these Nez Perce who slowly advanced as Whipple prepared his men to withstand the charge . . . but that assault never came. Not in the two hours his battalion held their ground on the side of that hill. For some reason that Whipple and Winters could not fathom, the warriors—who clearly outnumbered their soldiers—never pressed their advantage.

He shook his head as the Nez Perce mounted up and pulled back late that afternoon. "Should we withdraw, Captain?" Winters asked.

"We should continue our search for Lieutenant Rains," the captain replied. "But the enemy outnumbers us. I'm certain they will prevent us from advancing."

Winters regarded the lowering sun. "Might I suggest that we counter-march to Cottonwood?"

Whipple sighed, "We'll search for the bodies come morning."

Just before dusk, Whipple formed his battalion into a square around their horses, then slowly marched back to Cottonwood without having seen another Nez Perce throughout their retreat. As his battalion rode down into the wide gulch of the Cottonwood, he grew uneasy about their position, the fading light, and the close proximity of the enemy.

As night fell, he had his men establish a small defensive perimeter at the top of an adjacent hill where Whipple felt safer than down in the bottom with those gutted, abandoned, ghostly ranch buildings. Here at least they could command the high ground, able to see greater distances across the rolling Camas Prairie, too.

Not long after moonrise, the captain dispatched two couriers to carry word of the Rains affair to General Howard—the second leaving a half hour after the first.

> *Cottonwood, 10:30 P.M.*
>
> *(Tuesday)*
>
> *Joseph with his entire force is in our front. We moved out at 6 P.M. to look after the Indians reported. Rains, with ten men moved on ahead about two miles. We heard firing at the foot of the long hill back of Cottonwood, and mounting a slight elevation saw a large force of Indians occupying a strong position in the timber covering the road. Nothing could be seen of Rains and his party and we fear they have been slaughtered. We moved up close enough to see we were greatly outnumbered by enemies strongly posted. Night was approaching and after a consultation of all the officers it was decided to return to this place and hold it until Perry . . . should arrive. There was no diversity of opinion in this case, and there is no doubt that the entire command would have been sacrificed in an attack. We shall make every effort to communicate with Perry to-night and keep him out of any trap . . .*
>
> *Whipple, Cmd'g*
> *Cottonwood Station*

That done, Whipple had just begun to fitfully doze a little after midnight when a lone Christian tracker rode in, slipping down from the north.

"I'm amazed you got through from that direction!" the captain exclaimed as the friendly handed Whipple a folded letter. "That country was swarming with warriors earlier today."

In his dispatch, Captain David Perry informed whomever the courier would find in command of the closest outpost that he would be setting off from Fort Lapwai before first light with his supply train, moving south under a twenty-man escort.

"With the Nez Perce crawling across the countryside, we desperately need those supplies and especially that ammunition," Whipple told his officers he had called together in the starry darkness.

Lieutenant Shelton said, "I feel a bit uneasy about Colonel Perry, sir."

"To tell the truth, so do I," Whipple admitted. "Captain Winters, our entire battalion will depart at first light and march north to meet up with, and provide protection for, Colonel Perry's supply train."

"I'll see the men are awakened at five."

After his two army couriers returned after becoming lost in the darkened and unfamiliar terrain, Whipple himself spent the rest of that sleepless night waiting out the coming of the time when his noncoms would move among the enlisted, jarring them awake. No fires and no pipes. Which meant no coffee or fried bacon. Just a few crumbly bites of the inedible hardbread washed down with water from the Cottonwood before they moved out in the waning darkness of that morning, the anniversary of the nation's independence.

After crawling little more than two miles in the gray dawn, they stumbled across the remains of yesterday's massacre—at least, they found twelve of the thirteen bodies.

From their positions it was clear to see how the brief, hot fight had progressed. One body—of the civilian named Foster—was found in the tall grass, far out from the others. Then five more, soldiers all, scattered between the scout and those rocks where they located the last five, men who had attempted to sell their lives dearly. Empty copper cases glittered around them. But the weapons, gun belts, and their clothing were gone. And though the bodies had been stripped, none were mutilated or scalped.

"That's the lieutenant there, Captain," announced First Lieutenant Edwin H. Shelton. He would know. He and Rains were officers together in Whipple's L Company, First U. S. Cavalry.

Nonetheless, it was hard for the captain to believe that the disfigured body was that of young Rains.

"Appears the lieutenant really made the bastards angry," Whipple said quietly. "Look how many times they shot him before they finally caved in his skull."

"Shall we bury them here, sir?" Shelton asked.

Whipple regarded the climbing sun a moment, then answered, "No, Lieutenant. We can't help them now—but we must see what we can do to help Colonel Perry's escort. We'll push on."

Marching beyond the hillside where the Rains dead had taken refuge among those low boulders, Whipple's men spotted a solitary horse silhouetted atop a knoll, off to their right. Even with his field glasses, the captain was unable to determine if it was an Indian pony or one of the army horses claimed by those warriors who had committed the butchery on Lieutenant Rains.

"It could be one of ours, sir," Shelton reminded.

"I don't want to take the chance that it's a decoy," Whipple argued. "We won't be lured into an ambush as easily as others might."

Some six miles later the column he had deployed in double skirmish lines spotted Perry's seventy-five-mule supply train in the distance, its escort of twenty men from Company F, First U. S. Cavalry, just coming over the divide formed by nearby Craig's Mountain.

Perry patiently listened to Whipple's extensive report on the Rains affair, then put the captain at ease when he announced, "I'm assuming command of your entire outfit. We'll continue on in the direction of Cottonwood Station and reestablish our base there. On the way, we'll stop and bury your dead."

But upon retracing their steps to the boulders by midmorning, the Perry-Whipple command soon discovered the Nez Perce had returned in aggravating numbers. Enough marksmen began firing from the rocks and timber on the slope of Craig's Mountain that the burial details proved impossible. After close to an hour of long-distance sniping at the warriors, Perry ordered the efforts abandoned and they withdrew to Cottonwood.

Reaching the Norton ranch about noon, the combined battalion now boasted 113 men under arms. For the rest of that Fourth of July morning Perry, along with Whipple and Winters, supervised the digging of four long rifle pits, one arranged in a semicircle on a large hill immediately southeast of the Norton house, another in a semicircle on the height southwest of the house, along with barricades erected near the house and barn, constructed using the split rails taken from the fences they tore down, in addition to some native brown stone found in several piles around the ranch. One of the rifle pits that enjoyed the most commanding view of prairie for miles was backed up with one of Whipple's two Gatling guns.

The temperature continued to climb through the long summer morning, baking the men unmercifully as they toiled. The sun had reached midsky when the first picket hollered the alarm.

"Injuns! Injuns!"

Hurrying to the barricades at the northern side of their perimeter, Whipple was the first to watch the detail he had engaged to bury Lieutenant Rains turning back for the lines as several warriors approached the group from the upper reaches of Cottonwood Creek. As the soldiers watched from their rifle pits, more and more warriors arrayed themselves on the brow of the nearby hill, not far from where they had watched scout William Foster return at a gallop just yesterday. Some more gathered on another hill to the east and even more on the knoll just to the west, until the bivouac was completely surrounded by horsemen.

"How many of 'em?" some soldier asked.

"What the hell does it really matter, son?" growled civilian George M. Shearer. "There's more'n 'nough of the red niggers up there for all of us put together."

THE YANKEE SOLDIER who had lost them their fight in White Bird Canyon had assigned Shearer to supervise the construction of their fortifications at Norton's ranch. George was good at that. Lots of experience in that recent war against Yankee aggression.

But it seemed strange that he would be put in charge of so important a task when Colonel Perry had officers in his command who might have just as much experience building such defenses. But, George thought with a wry grin, while he and the poor enlisted men were up here on the heights digging the rifle pits, most every one of Perry's officers were down there in the gulch near the station buildings, idle as could be, not occupied with a damned thing.

Shearer had come in from Mount Idaho late that morning with three friends, having received word that there were soldiers at Cottonwood who might be in need of reinforcements. Four men weren't much, but every man with a gun could well mean several more dead Indians by the end of a skirmish. Besides, if there was any chance of cutting down some more of those redskins, George was the first to mount up and ride into the fray.

Back when the outbreak was just getting under way, Shearer had put together a posse of twenty volunteers to go in search of any additional survivors after the raid on the Norton party. He had rallied them into action, reminding his group of the pitiful sight of that Chamberlin woman as she scrambled away from her rescuers like a terrified animal, reminding them, too, of the wounded, inhuman cries that had escaped her throat.

"Ain't none of us ever gonna forget the sight of that poor Mrs. Chamberlin, fellers," he had drawled in that distinctive Southern manner of his, something unique that set him apart from most others here in the Northwest, "knowing full well what them red Neegras done to her again and again: a fate that's nigh wuss'n death."

Such treatment of women and children was enough to lather a gentleman something fierce.

"So let's go see 'bout catching us some red bucks and chopping off their balls afore we kill 'em real slow!" Shearer had goaded his band of twenty, shaking his double-barreled Parker shotgun over his head.

Little wonder he was worked up by the time they got the jump on a trio of Nez Perce bucks out at Ab Smith's place. That set George to whooping with something akin to the Rebel yell, partly growling like that big black-haired mastiff one of the shopkeepers kept chained up outside his trading tent in the mining camp of Florence. Why, he sounded just like a snarling dog ready to lunge and latch onto your leg, take a hunk of meat right out of your arm . . . maybe even clamp its jaws down your throat—if you were a Nez Perce.

While two of the trio had leaped their horses over a fence, the third dismounted and started to hobble away. The posse shot the warrior several times before George halted over the Indian's body and unloaded one of the two barrels into his back, so close the black powder started the Indian's shirt to smoldering. But when he discovered the buck's hand still twitching, Shearer had dismounted and inverted his shotgun, slamming the buttstock down into the warrior's head. With a second blow, George shattered the stock.

"Goddamn, if that didn't feel good!" Shearer roared triumphantly, shaking his blood-splattered double-barreled shotgun in glee.

"Bet this son of a bitch was one of them what got to Chamberlin's woman!" one of the posse had cheered.

"This'un prob'ly killed that li'l girl, too," another voice chimed in.

A third man had growled, "Likely this bastard chopped off the other girl's tongue!"

The killing of that lone warrior had in no way cooled the unmitigated fury Shearer felt at the Nez Perce for what they'd done to those women and children they had attacked out on the Camas Road. And the army's defeat at the White Bird only added more heat to his bloodlust for those less-than-human warriors who could commit such savage acts against the innocent.

Maybe now, here at Cottonwood—he brooded—they could finally pit themselves against these red sonsabitches in a stand-up, man-to-man fight.

CHAPTER SEVENTEEN

———◄═◆═►———

Khoy-Tsahl, 1877

THE DAY WE CELEBRATE.
———

The nation will celebrate to-day the one
hundred and first anniversary of the declaration
of independence. The first century with its record
of heroic achievement and splendid growth has closed,
and we stand inside the threshold of the second. The
war of the revolution, the second conflict with England,
the conquest of Mexico, the determined struggle for the
union, the social, industrial, moral, commercial and
political progress of the first hundred years of
national existence, with all their proud memories and
patriotic reminiscences, are now matters of a past
century,—to be recalled on each recurring anniversary,
to impress their lessons of duty and patriotism upon
every citizen of the republic . . .
—editorial
Rocky Mountain News
July 4, 1877

SHORE CROSSING COULD SEE THAT THE SOLDIER CHIEF WAS CONTENT TO fight nothing more than a defensive skirmish through the rest of that long, hot afternoon. Evidently, the *suapie* saw no need to order his men out of their deep holes and charge off in pursuit of all those warriors who had them surrounded. In their hollows,* those soldiers were far safer than the soldiers had been at *Lahmotta.*

For the most part, the *Nee-Me-Poo* also seemed content to harass the *suapies,* staying on their ponies, just out of range of the Shadow guns, riding this way and that around the entire circle of the soldier camp while a long-distance duel was waged throughout the long summer afternoon. But a few men dismounted from time to time, creeping up through the grass, often slipping as close as two arrow flights to the hollows, hidden by the brush

---

*The term the Nez Perce veterans historically used to describe the rifle pits in their testimony on the Cottonwood skirmishes after the war.

choking the ravines, until they were discovered—when they were either driven back by soldier bullets or forced to keep their heads down, stalled in their skulking.

Just before dusk Rainbow called for an attack on the southwestern edge of the *suapie* lines. But before the mounted charge could get very close, the soldiers turned their wagon gun[*] on the horsemen, hitting four of the ponies and turning back their daring assault. At times through the day, one or more of the horses were hit, here or there around the huge circle, but no man was ever struck by a bullet. There were no wounded or killed in that hot, noisy fight.

Those soldiers had no idea that the *Nee-Me-Poo* weren't fighting to dislodge the white men dug in like frightened gophers. No, this skirmishing with a lot of noise and yelling but no killing was only a diversion being conducted to keep the *suapies* busy while the camp inched across the naked, barren prairie just behind the northern hills. The men were buying time for their families, women, and children to escape down the Cottonwood to the Clearwater, where they could join up with the Looking Glass people.

They kept up their shooting until it grew dark; then Rainbow and Five Wounds had their warriors mount up. They rode off to rejoin the village.

And when the sun rose tomorrow, there might be some more long-distance skirmishing to keep the soldiers in their holes while the village finished its journey across the rolling prairie. This diversionary tactic had been decided by the Non-Treaty bands at a council held all the way back on the west side of the *Tahmonah* two days ago.

Finding that Cut-Off Arm was indeed determined to follow them into that high, rugged, muddy country, the chiefs hurried the people north until they reached the familiar crossing at Luke Billy's place.[**] But before ordering their people into their bullboats once again, the chiefs met in a hastily called council to decide where they would be going once they had crossed the river. North, east, or south? To the north lay the friendly Cayuse but also the Flathead, who might prove troublesome to the Non-Treaty bands because they were so closely allied with the Shadows. Over to the east lay the buffalo country that Looking Glass knew so well—but to reach it they would need Looking Glass's help. And to the south lay a route that, Joseph explained, would take his Wallamwatkin people back in the direction of their ancestral hunting grounds.

"I wish to stay close to my homeland," the Wallowa chief told the assembly. "If we need to fight, my heart tells me to fight the war in our own country. To fight *for* our own country."

Listening to the other chiefs, Shore Crossing was thankful White Bird and *Toohoolhoolzote* spoke on behalf of turning east and fighting their way across the Camas Prairie. A good thing the fighting chiefs outnumbered the Wallowa leader in the arguments made in that council. Joseph was silenced

---

[*]Whipple's Gatling gun.
[**]Craig Billy Crossing.

when White Bird announced that they would cross the river and march in search of Looking Glass on the Clearwater.

Over the past two days of fighting the *suapies*, first in the rocks and later from their dug-out hollows, Shore Crossing had been reminded how most of the warriors really felt about Joseph. That soft-spoken orator had taken no part in the fight at *Lahmotta*. Instead, his brother, *Ollokot*—called the Frog in his childhood—had dashed out to join in humiliating and routing the soldiers.

Every one of the fighting men who had listened in on that fateful council among the chiefs before crossing the river believed that Joseph should leave the fighting decisions up to the war leaders. His words and wishes shunned on the west bank of the Salmon, Joseph had been relegated to an even more subordinate role.

It made Shore Crossing grin to think how this Wallowa who had spoken so strongly against the struggle at its start, was now helplessly swept up in that war, overshadowed by real fighting men. *Eeh! Let Joseph take care of the women and children and sick ones! Leave to this camp chief only those decisions no more important than those made by a herder!*

Yet one thing remained a constant: The *suapies* would follow the village. They always followed. Which meant that the real fighting was yet to come.

Shore Crossing didn't think he could wait for the blooding.

"COUNT ME IN, Cap'n Randall!" cheered thirty-eight-year-old Luther P. Wilmot as he scrambled up to join the small group gathered around D. B. Randall in front of Loyal P. Brown's Mount Idaho House hotel.

"I'm proud to have you ride with us, Lew!" answered Darius B. Randall, the popular leader of the civilian militia recently banded together, what with the Nez Perce uprising. He himself had a long-standing dispute with the peaceful Treaty bands, who claimed Randall was illegally squatting on their reservation.

"I ain't got no horse, 'cept that wagon puller brung me in when Pete and me was jumped on the Cottonwood Road," Wilmot apologized in his soft voice, brushing some of the dirty blond hair out of an eye.

"One of you boys fetch Lieutenant Wilmot a saddle," Randall asked the crowd, then looked at Lew again.

"L-lieutenant?" Wilmot echoed the rank.

Randall nodded. "You're a steady hand, Lew. We're gonna get in a fight with these redskins soon enough. Something happens to the captain of this outfit, they're gonna need a lieutenant—a steady hand—to keep 'em together. Besides Jim Cearly over there—you fit the bill nicely, Lieutenant."

"T-thanks, D. B.," he answered quietly, a little self-conscious in front of the other men.

"Now go get that big horse you rode in here," Randall suggested. "That wagon puller of yours was strong enough to get you to Mount Idaho just in front of them Injuns. It'll be strong enough to carry you on that scout I want you to lead over west to Lawyer's Canyon."

This first morning after Independence Day, a Thursday, Randall was calling for volunteers to join him in going to relief of the army entrenched on Cottonwood Creek.

For the last two or three days news had been drifting in that the hostiles had recrossed the Salmon River and were slowly marching for the Clearwater, with the likely intention of joining up with the survivors of Whipple's botched attack on Looking Glass's village.

Wilmot and his handful of scouts hadn't gotten but a couple of miles out of town, making for Lawyer's Canyon on the far side of Craig's Divide, when they met a Camas Prairie settler, who told them the hostiles had in fact reached the east side of the Salmon and were crossing behind Craig's Mountain.

"I was up to the soldier camp at Ben Norton's ranch last couple of days," Dan Crooks explained. "Told them the news, too. To see for themselves, the officers sent out a scouting party two days back, with near twice as many men as you got with you, Lew."

"Them soldiers see the Nez Perce camp like you done?"

Crooks wagged his head dolefully. " All of 'em got wiped out."

Of a sudden, Lew remembered how the body of John Chamberlin had looked when they found him on the prairie. "Massacred?"

"Soldiers went right out that evening to bring back them butchered bodies, but on the way back to Cottonwood they was jumped by an even bigger war party and was drove back to Norton's about nightfall," Crooks declared.

Lew studied the face of this youngest son of John W. Crooks, a wealthy landowner in these parts. "Them Injuns move on?"

Crooks wagged his head. "They come right back yesterday for a long fight with the soldiers; noon till moonrise, it was. So last evening I decided I was gonna light out for Mount Idaho at sunrise this here morning—gonna bring word to my pa and everybody that them soldiers need a hand."

"C'mon," said the lean and lanky Wilmot as he reined his horse around. "We're going back to tell Captain Randall your bad news. I figger he'll want us all to light out for Cottonwood Station to give the army some help."

If anything was going to be done about stopping that Nez Perce village marching east from Craig's Mountain, then they would need every man—soldier *and* civilian—to get the job done.

Lew Wilmot and his twenty-eight-year-old freighting partner, Peter H. Ready, had had their own run-in with some murderous Nez Perce out on the Cottonwood Road just twenty days before, the same night the Nortons and Chamberlins were jumped and most in the escaping party killed. But the pair of teamsters had managed to cut free a couple of their big harness horses and lumber off bareback while most of the warriors slowed and halted to rummage through all those supplies destined for the Vollmer and Scott store in Mount Idaho the white men had been hauling in their two wagons. Up to that moment, neither of them had heard a thing of what trouble was then afoot. An outright Indian uprising.

So this morning when Randall issued his call for volunteers, Wilmot could think of nothing more than his Louisa and their four young children. Brooding not only about the aging and infirm father he was caring for, as well as his wife, Louisa, and their three daughters . . . Lew's thoughts were also all wrapped up in that two-day-old son Louisa had just given him. What sort of place would this be if the Nez Perce weren't driven back onto their reservation? How would life on the Camas Prairie go on if this bloody uprising wasn't put down and the murderers hung? Lew Wilmot had to do what he could to make this country safe for women and children.

He had come here from Illinois when he was but a lad himself—his father marching the family to Oregon on that long Emigrant Road. Not once in all those years growing up in this very country had Lew ever done one goddamned thing against these Cayuse or Palouse or the Nez Perce. But . . . the way they had screamed for his blood during that dark night's horse race across the prairie sure convinced Lew those warriors had some score to settle with somebody.

Lew and Pete had lost just about everything when they lost their freight, those two big wagons, and the rest of their draft animals to the war party.

"But we got our hair, Pete," Lew had reminded his younger partner as they reached the barricades at Mount Idaho in the inky blackness. "Just remember that: We still got our goddamn hair."

When Wilmot carried the news of the skirmishing at Cottonwood back to Randall, the captain announced he would be leaving for Norton's ranch within the hour.

"Lew! Lew!"

Wilmot turned as he finished tying off the horse to the hitching post outside Loyal P. Brown's hotel. It was a red-faced Benjamin F. Evans, a local.

"You coming along, Ben?"

"I'd like to go, but don't have no horse."

Turning slightly, Wilmot patted the rump of his horse and said, "Listen here—I've got a friend who owns one of the best horses on Camas Prairie, and he told me any time I went out for some scouting I could have his horse to ride. You can ride this'un here, and I'll go fetch that other'un for myself."

Although twenty-five men had offered to ride with Randall earlier that morning, only fourteen others answered D. B.'s call, joining Wilmot and Evans when they rose to the saddle a half hour later, all seventeen starting out of Mount Idaho for Cottonwood. Lew looked around him at the others. At least ten were joking and slapping at one another, acting like this was going to be some Fourth of July church picnic.

At the same time all Lew could think about were those three girls of his, Louisa, and that two-day-old baby boy—the five of them taking cover back there in Loyal P.'s hotel.

Cottonwood lay some sixteen miles off across the gently rolling Camas Prairie. A lot of bare, goddamned open ground to his way of thinking.

"CAPTAIN WHIPPLE!"

He turned on his heel at the cry.

"Two riders coming in—at a gallop!"

Stephen Whipple could see how those men licked it down the road from Mount Idaho. Clearly soldiers, the yellow cavalry stripes on their britches aglitter in the summer sunlight that late morning, their stirrups bobbing with every heaving lunge the horses made, hooves kicking up scuffs of dust as they tore down the aching green of the Camas Prairie.

"They're gonna have trouble now, Captain!" announced Second Lieutenant William H. Miller, pointing off to the east, where a war party of some twenty warriors suddenly popped over a low rise. A half-dozen of them immediately reined aside and started angling in a lope toward the two couriers while the rest came to a halt to watch the attack.

As soon as this news was reported to Captain David Perry, the commander ordered half of L Company to saddle their mounts and prepare to go to the aid of that endangered pair of riders.

"How far off do you take them to be, Lieutenant?" Whipple asked Miller, who had his field glasses pressed against his nose.

"Two miles, Captain. No more than that."

Whipple turned at the rumble of hooves as those mounted cavalrymen rattled past at a walk, then broke into a lope as soon as they cleared the outer rifle pits. A quarter of a mile away the detail halted and shifted into a broad front, removing their carbines from the short slings worn over their shoulders. As the soldiers at Cottonwood watched, puffs of dirty gray smoke appeared above the detail. Then, two seconds later, the loud reports reached the bivouac. Volley by volley, the rescue detail was shooting over the heads of the couriers, laying their fire down at those six pursuing warriors.

"It worked, Captain!" Miller cried. "By damn, it worked, sir!"

Whipple only nodded, his attention suddenly snagged on something else. "Let me see those glasses, Lieutenant."

Miller handed the binoculars to him. Putting them to his eyes, Whipple slowly twisted the adjustment wheel, bringing the distant figures into focus.

The lieutenant asked, "More Indians, Captain?"

"I'm not really sure," Whipple replied. "They don't look to be riding like Indians. And they're coming across the Prairie from Mount Idaho."

"How many? Can you tell, sir?"

"Less than two dozen," the captain said. "No more than twenty at the most."

"With news from us about the Rains defeat," Miller began, "would General Howard be sending us any reinforcements from his column?"

"No—I think that's a band of civilians, Lieutenant."

Then Whipple slowly dragged his field of vision to the right, scanning the Camas Prairie just west of the Cottonwood–Mount Idaho Road. But he stopped, held, took a breath as he twisted the adjustment wheel.

"The village is on the move, gentlemen."

Out in the lead of the distant mass were the horses, two—maybe as many as three—thousand of them. As he watched, Whipple's heart sank.

Sixty, seventy, shit—more than a hundred horsemen began peeling away from both sides of the column now, feathers and bows and rifles bristling atop their painted, racing ponies. More than a hundred-twenty of them now made their appearance from the backside of Craig's Mountain. And instead of coming for Perry's bivouac at Cottonwood, they were angling off for that small group of horsemen coming out from Mount Idaho.

Whipple moved his view back to the south, finding those civilians once more, as the massive war party put their ponies into a gallop.

"Something tells me those riders aren't soldiers," the captain declared. "I figure them for a band of hapless civilians whose luck has just run out."